THE KING OF STARLIGHT

BRIANA BLYE

The King of Starlight

Author: Briana Blye
Date of Publication: November 2025
Copyright © 2025

Copyright © 2025 Briana Blye

All rights reserved. No part of this book may be reproduced, stored in a retrieval system, or transmitted in any form or by any means: electronic, mechanical, photocopying, recording, or otherwise, without the prior written permission of the author, except in the case of brief quotations embodied in critical articles or reviews.

This is a work of fiction. Names, characters, businesses, places, events, and incidents are either the products of the author's imagination or used in a fictitious manner. Any resemblance to actual persons, living or dead, or actual events is purely coincidental.

First Edition: November 2025

Published by Briana Blye

Printed in the United States of America

Cover Design by Briana Blye

Edited by Briana Blye

ABOUT THE AUTHOR

Briana Blye is a fantasy author drawn to magical worlds, romantic tension, and stories where the impossible feels just within reach. Inspired by fantasy, romantasy, and fae lore, she finds herself lost in enchanted forests, ancient magic, and otherworldly realms.

When she's not writing, Briana can be found with a cup of coffee, her cat and chickens close by, or wandering through nature—where the world still feels a little magical.

amazon.com/author/brianablye
goodreads.com/authorbrianablye
bookbub.com/profile/briana-blye

PROLOGUE

In some worlds, the darkness is powerful. In others, the light never fades. The world of Nyriathee is no exception.

Here, forests grow without end; stars shift their constellations nightly, and the sky stretches vast and eternal. The land belongs to the *Fae of Nyriathee*, who bathe in starlight°° and wield powerful magic of enchantment and trickery. Fields ripple with silver grass that hums in harmony with the wind. Waterfalls cascade in iridescent ribbons. Crystal-laced trees pulse with their heartbeat. Above, the skies shift in golden and rose-tinted waves, while the air is thick with the scent of star petals and lilac.

Yet beneath the beauty lie strict laws, for the Fae live by three unbreakable rules:

1. *The debt must be balanced.*

2. *A name is a blade.*

3. *Do not invite the eyes of humans, unless for one's own entertainment.*

But not all Fae believe they must abide by the rules.

Fae of every kind roam. Some wear the shapes of humans, but never as humans truly are. Their faces are flawless, untouched by the scars, lines, or blemishes that mark human life. Their eyes gleam too brightly, their smiles cut too sharp. Their glamour is a mask that only some can see through, if they're lucky. Others move with the grace of animals, though they are beasts made strange with antlers, wings stitched with shadow, claws that glint like crystal. Stranger still are those who look as though they were born from the depths, forms so alien they unmake the very idea of flesh and bone. Where humans are fragile, flawed, and fleeting, the Fae are unsettling in their perfection. To stand among them is to be reminded that mortality itself is imperfection. Mortality is soft, unguarded, and painfully real.

Fae alliances here are fragile. Betrayal is currency.

The realm of the Nyriathee Fae is contradiction made flesh: lush yet deadly, radiant yet cruel. It is no place for human hearts. Humans who stumble through hidden doorways or fall beneath moonlit glamours seldom return. The land of Nyriathee does not forgive. It does not forget. It is beauty sharpened into a blade.

The landscape itself is ever-changing, molded by the will of the King who rules the *Court of Starlight*. Forests bloom overnight in impossible colors—black leaves veined with gold, bark inscribed with glowing runes. Lakes shimmer with illusions, reflecting not the sky but a thousand possible futures. Mountains sing with the breath of slumbering magic.

Time is not constant here. A single step into Nyriathee may cost a human a year...or a hundred. Lovers have wandered in chasing whispers and emerged hollow-eyed centuries later, forgotten by their bloodlines. Children taken by the Fae return crowned in thorns, smiles too wide, eyes too ancient. Almost unrecognizable to their true human form. To the fae, humans are soft things. They are fascinating, foolish, and fleeting. Humans are welcomed only as entertainment, bargaining chips, prey, or pets. Those who dare strike bargains are bound by contracts carved in starlight and sealed with something deeper than blood. There is no mercy in this land. Magic thrives on intent, and beauty is its sharpest weapon. Even flowers can bite. The wind itself carries voices not meant for human ears.

Above all sits the King of the Nyriathee: ruler of the Court of Starlight. *King Corvin* is as devious as moonlight and twice as cold. His crown is woven from star-gold, old, cracked bones, and the petals of a long-dead starflower. His throne is made from black crystal that drinks starlight itself, drawing every mote of brilliance toward him as though the heavens bow in eternal reverence. His magic shimmers with constellations, flickering like a dying sun, bending the very laws of nature. When he walks, starlight spills in his wake—an argent glow that illuminates nothing, only deepens the shadows. Across his back rests a mighty silver sword, its blade kissed by fallen stars and stained with blood that never fades. He does not rule by fear, but by the silence that follows it. Even the most ruthless Fae bow when his shadow falls across them like an eclipse. To disobey him is to write one's death sentence among the constellations.

King Corvin is a creature of control, temptation, and desire. His heart is a black star that pulls all into its orbit.

In Nyriathee, nothing is ever what it seems. And everything has a cost.

CHAPTER I
THE HOLLOW LANDS

"Liora!"

I glanced up at my younger sister's voice. She leaned out the second-floor window, elbows resting carefully on the sill. "Don't be gone too late. Mom said she gets worried when you walk at night."

I rolled my eyes, but couldn't hide a smile. "I do this all the time. I'll be fine."

She pressed her forehead against the screen. "I know. But you *know* how she is."

Worried. Always worried.

My family isn't perfect, but they're loving. Money is always tight. My father works two jobs, construction most days, and landscaping rich people's houses on weekends. He never complains; I think he even enjoys it. My mother is a second grade school teacher, and writes poetry in every spare moment, lecturing us like students one day and spending the next hunched over her laptop, fingers flying. They're busy, but always caring.

That means my sister and I have each other. We play video games, binge-watch shows, get dressed up to go nowhere, and raid

1

the kitchen late at night when the house is quiet. Over the years, friends drifted away, but my sister never has. I'm nineteen now, and my sister is sixteen, but the age difference never mattered to us. We resemble each other enough that no one doubts we're sisters, though not so much that we're mistaken for twins. Elsie's hair is a soft blonde, threaded with faint shimmers of red, and she has our mother's hazel eyes and our father's nose. My own hair falls long and dark, the color of rich chocolate, with my father's blue eyes and my mother's nose. Elsie has always felt like a part of me I could never live without. My sister is, and always will be, my best friend.

The streetlamps buzzed to life as I stepped off the porch, their light barely pushing back the deepening shadows. Nights in our neighborhood always carried a strange hush, as if the world held its breath when the sun went down. It could be eerie at times, but mostly I enjoyed it.

Crickets sang from the garden nearby and somewhere far off a dog barked, but the silence between sounds felt a bit heavier than normal. I thought about turning back to the safety of home, but something called to me. Something I couldn't yet explain.

I pulled my old brown jacket tighter around me, the worn leather creaking softly in protest. Beneath it, my faded flannel brushed against my skin, the fabric smelling faintly of smoke and pine. My cold, ring-covered hands disappeared into the deep pockets, metal clinking softly as I walked. The worn knees of my jeans brushed together with each step, and my boots crunched over the ground as I followed the rough path that cut between the dark woods and town. It wasn't far, but my mom hated it when I went there after dark. She said strange things had happened in those woods, and though it had been a while since anything new, the possibility still lingered.

When I was younger, my mother used to tell me stories. They were half warnings, half confessions of events that happened to people from her own childhood. One was about a boy who wandered off and was later found deep in the pine trees, eyes wide and unblinking as though he hadn't slept in weeks. The news claimed he'd possibly been drugged, or something just as awful. His eyes would weep continuously, and he had this strange smell of burning wood and salt water that they couldn't get out of his clothes or out of his hair. He survived, but he couldn't explain what happened. His memory was gone, scrubbed clean as if the forest itself had stolen it.

My mother once confessed that she, too, had wandered into Silver Pine Forest when she was young. She claimed she was driven by curiosity, or perhaps by the same unseen pull that lured so many before her. She told me the forest hoarded secrets, guarding them with jealousy, sharing only scraps with those who listened closely. Whispers, she said, so faint they threaded through the leaves like breath—whispers only those born of magic could truly understand. She spoke of creatures that gathered in hidden spaces to revel on the solstices, and of soil that shifted beneath her feet as though the land itself were alive, trembling like an earthquake. She once told me that, in her late teens, she'd been drawn to the forest in ways she could never quite explain. She would walk the path beneath daylight's safety, but return again when the moon rose high, claiming the woods in silver light. She said the stars seemed brighter there, almost as if they were closer to her somehow—as if they were listening. The air shimmered with a quiet pulse that felt alive, familiar, like it recognized her. Sometimes, her name would drift through the branches, soft as starlight, carried by a voice she could never find. When she spoke of those nights, her gaze would always lift skyward, as though searching for something she'd left among the constellations. I used to laugh at her tales, dismissing them as fanciful warnings meant to keep me from straying too far. Yet, on nights when the moon burned a little too bright or the air grew still enough to silence even the crickets, I caught myself wondering if the tales she told me weren't just simple stories, but that they had some truth behind them.

But one story clung to me more than the rest. She told me there was a girl from Elmcrest High School who disappeared into the forest one evening. She was only fifteen years old and had been walking with friends, talking and laughing about boys and school. Her friends said she seemed fine, and when one of them turned to her, she was gone. They swore she hadn't screamed, hadn't even made a sound. One moment she was there, the next she wasn't.

And the worst part was, she never came back.

Rumors spread. Some said maybe she'd run away or maybe she'd been pulled off the path. Some whispered about a serial killer, others about kidnappers, but nothing was ever proven. The police worked endlessly, trying to uncover clues and holding search parties for her, but nothing surfaced. A few even muttered that her friends knew more than they let on, but no evidence of that was ever found. No answers. Just silence, thick as the one that hangs over the land after snowfall. My mother said a dark cloud hung over the town for years until her family moved away. People tried to go back to life as before, but things were never the same.

I wasn't nervous though. I had gone for night walks ever since I was fourteen. Sometimes I'd go with friends, my mother, Elsie, or by myself. I felt drawn to the forest in strange ways. Maybe it was the smell of damp earth after the sun went down, my mother's stories, or the restless stirrings of creatures hidden in the brush. There was a rhythm to it all, as if the woods were breathing in their own time. It felt unnaturally exciting, as if the forest knew me and needed me in a way I couldn't explain. Sometimes, when the wind shifted just right, I swore I could hear the faintest sound of my name rising from between the trees, as if the forest carried my name in a song no one else could hear. It unsettled me and comforted me at the same time, like a lullaby sung in a language I didn't know.

The closer I came to the tree line, the more the world behind me seemed to fade. The buzzing streetlamps, the chatter of distant televisions, and the ordinary weight of home...it all slipped away, leaving me alone with the hush of the forest waiting. My steps slowed, but I didn't stop. I couldn't. The shadows were deep, yes, but they felt like open arms. And so, like I always did, I crossed the threshold, a brave smile on my face, my eyes sharp and watching.

The night sky sparkled with a rich, velvety blue, and golden stars glittered just above the tree tops. An owl hooted above, a soft song to welcome the night as it swept through the trees and over the land. The forest floor was damp beneath my feet, and moss clung to the trees as it glimmered softly in the moonlight. I was familiar with the forest at night, delving into late-night walks and whispering to the shadows that surrounded me. The forest made me feel whole. It made me feel alive. It's as if we were connected somehow, enjoying the company of one another. The wind whispered my name, and I whispered back.

A small, orange flame danced atop the white candle in my right hand as I walked. The path ahead of me was swallowed in darkness, but the candlelight was just enough to keep my steps steady. The creatures of the forest greeted me with a sense of familiarity and friendship. It was as if we understood one another. They'd investigate me, scurrying along the forest floor or nestled in their homes, watching me from the trees high above. The forest creatures and I were quiet, secretive, and learned to navigate the darkness using our senses. Overhead, a bat swept low between the branches, a blur of motion.

As I walked, I listened to the cool wind blow between the trees and down the dirt path ahead of me. The leaves rustled together, the crickets chirped, owls sang, and a coyote howled as a warning of attack or content. Something in the bushes to my right moved, followed by a low, unfamiliar hiss. I paused and held the candle closer to the bushes, hoping to illuminate the creature making the sound.

"Hello?" I whispered, "I'm Liora. I'm not going to hurt you."

The hissing grew louder as if alerting me that danger was near. I remembered my mother's stories. Her warnings. I remembered the young girl who had vanished and never returned. I took a deep breath, trying to ground myself. I wondered if this was what she heard before she disappeared.

The hiss came again, this time as if it were directly into my right ear. It startled me, the candle in my hand crashing to the dirt. The hissing deepened into a vibration beneath my feet, and the ground gave a subtle lurch, as though gravity had shifted sideways. My ears popped, and the night air thickened, heavy with a sweetness that didn't belong here. My heart pounded with chaos, and my mother's stories seemed more realistic than ever. The trees wavered, their trunks bending as though reflected in rippling water. The shadows of the branches stretched too long, curling like grasping fingers toward the edge of the cliff. The soil trembled, and for a moment it felt as though the cliff was breathing beneath me, exhaling warmth from some cavernous depth. Pebbles skittered away from my boots, rattling into the abyss, but I never heard them strike bottom. The air seemed to follow them downward, tugging at the hem of my pants like invisible hands.

The candle's flame sputtered, and in its last flicker, I glimpsed a forest below. It was not a reflection, but another world yawning open in the depths. Its trees gleamed silver in the dark, their branches swaying. The earth shivered again, urging me closer to the edge as though it was no longer solid ground but a threshold.

"No!" I gasped, dropping to my knees, fingers scrambling through the dirt. The candle's glow was gone, and with it, my anchor to the night. My knees scraped raw against the soil as my fingers dug in frantic circles, cold earth packing beneath my nails. Panic tightened in my chest, seeping into my skin with the chill of the ground.

After several desperate minutes, I forced myself to stand, dragging a breath into my lungs. I had walked these woods plenty of times, listening to the trees, guided by the river's song. The silver moonlight should be enough to lead me home. I took a few careful steps forward, arms outstretched, reaching into the dark. My palms pressed against the damp bark, cool against the burning sting of my scraped skin. Slowly, my breath began to steady.

"You'll be okay," I whispered to myself. "You know this forest, and the forest knows you."

But the forest felt different tonight. The air was heavy, humid, and syrup-thick against my ribs. The ground gave a subtle shiver beneath my boots, a low vibration that rose into my bones. I froze. The silence was too deep, too watchful, until a sudden snap of a twig echoed behind me.

My heart lurched. I spun, too fast, my foot catching on loose soil. The earth seemed to tilt, tugging me forward with a force that wasn't entirely gravity. Pebbles scattered from beneath my boots, vanishing into a depth that swallowed sound. My arms flailed, searching for balance, for something solid to cling to, but I found only air.

Tripping. Falling. Tumbling into the void yawning beneath the cliff. The blackness of the night swallowed me whole. As I plummeted, the world slowed, and my eyes caught a flicker of movement above. It was a strange figure leaning over the edge. Human-shaped, yes, but not quite human. Its skin, pale green like new leaves after rain, seemed to catch the moonlight and shimmer faintly. For an instant, the wind carried with it the scent of moss and jasmine, sharp and sweet, as though the forest itself had followed me into the abyss. Then the darkness closed in, and the creature was gone.

CHAPTER 2
THE FALL

The feeling of falling was terrifying. I couldn't even comprehend exactly what had happened. One moment the ground was steady beneath me, and the next it shifted, crumbling away like it had been waiting for me to take another step. My body slid, dirt and stones scraping against my skin as gravity claimed me, tumbling me down into the dark. My breath was torn from my throat in a silent scream. The world blurred into a rush of shadow and sound, and for a moment I wasn't sure if I was moving or the darkness itself was swallowing me whole.

That face—the pale green face that watched me fall was burned behind my eyes. Its hollow expression, unblinking and almost curious, lingered in my mind even as I fell further, faster. I tried to reach out, to grasp something solid, but my fingers ran over small rocks, dirt, and closed on nothing but air. Then the thought came, cold and clear through the chaos: *I must already be dead.*

When I opened my eyes, cold drops of water splashed against my face. The air felt warmer, sticky with humidity. The silver moonlight still filtered through the trees, but the stars had changed. They were no longer the familiar gold, but shimmered with a soft pink hue. It was unlike anything I had ever seen. I raised my hand, rubbing my throbbing head as a sharp headache pulsed through my skull. With a fall like that, I knew I must be dead.

"That was quite a fall," a deep voice rang out from the space around me.

The pounding in my head blurred my senses, making it difficult to discern the source of the voice.

"Another human from Silver Pine Forest," the deep voice said again, followed by a low, eerie chuckle. "Humans are so, so, strange."

I rolled onto my side and gathered what little strength I had left to push myself to my feet. Sticks and dirt clung to my tangled hair as I rubbed my eyes, coughing. The aching of my body felt too real. I couldn't have been dead. If I were, I wouldn't feel anything. Right?

"Wet, oily skin, no fur, and short, useless nails," the voice rang out once more, echoing through the night, "What a pity, what a shame."

The voice was deep, masculine even. Concern tugged at my chest, nervous about the aching of my own body, and cautious about who the face was behind the voice I was hearing.

"Who are you?" I asked, pulling the crunchy, dry leaves from my dirty hair. "And why are you wandering in the forest so late at night?"

"This is *my* forest," the voice sneered, a hint of mystery in their tone. "You are not in the same *human* forest you came from, Liora."

My breath caught in my throat.

I rubbed my eyes with my fingers. "How do you know my name?" I whispered, searching for the owner of the voice, my head still pounding with defeat.

A soft rustle sounded behind me, like leaves stirred by a breeze that hadn't touched my skin. I thought it might be the strange-looking creature I had seen before I fell. Its skin, pale green and sickly-looking. I turned slowly and to my surprise, I saw tall, silver-barked trees laced with glowing green vines that pulsed like veins. The air was still humid and thick against my heavy lungs. It smelt like wet dirt after a rainstorm, like the world itself was underwater.

Then I saw him.

He was leaning against the trunk of a twisted tree as if it had grown just to cradle him there. He was tall and shockingly so, his stature ethereal as if divinity itself had taken human form for a fleeting moment. He stood as though he had never once needed to assert his power; it simply existed around him, within him. His features were flawless, as though carved by the gods, with centuries of devotion poured into their sculpting. His hair was as dark as raven feathers, thick and tousled, with strands that shimmered violet under the dying light. Two small, pointy ears were partially hidden in the mess of his hair, elegant and poised.

But it was his eyes that honestly struck me. They were golden, glowing faintly through the mist like stars, framed by thick lashes and impossibly sharp cheekbones. If I weren't mistaken, I would have thought I was dreaming or dead. His presence was stunning, too beautiful to be safe, and the air around him buzzed with static.

He wore a cloak of deep blue, the edges of which were embroidered with golden thread that caught the pink gleam of the sky. It looked like something a person of honor would wear. His lips curled up on the sides as he watched me closely, an evil smirk on his face. His ears, tapered like a fox's, twitched toward me beneath a delicate crown, slightly tilted. The crown was crafted from gold and bone, featuring rare and intricate flower petals that appeared like jewels etched into it. He leaned against a sword, pressed sharply into the dirt, creating a deep hole where it stood.

His skin was slightly tan, much different than the creature I had seen while free-falling. There was a small patch of blood that trickled down his rosy cheek, but still, he stood as if the pain of the cut did not bother him. He wiped the dark liquid away with ease, and it was obvious that he bore only a few creature-like traits, yet there was no mistaking that he wasn't entirely human and made no effort to pretend otherwise. Captivated by his horrifically beautiful presence, I couldn't look away.

A knowing smile spread across his face. "I make it my business to know the names of those who enter my kingdom, my realm, and my court."

I gave him a puzzled look, unsure of how to respond.

Obviously aware of my confusion, he cleared his throat, "It's strange, you know, this has never happened before...not quite like this."

"Huh?" I breathed, feeling more confused the more he spoke, "What hasn't happened before?" I felt myself choke on the heavy words in my throat, "Am I...am I dead?"

"Your name," he said, tilting his head as he looked at me. "It came whispered by the trees long before you arrived. Well, before you fell." He paused before chuckling gently, "Death is not welcome here unless by my own hands, or by those whom I allow to summon it."

"Arrived? Whispered by the trees?" I questioned, glancing around frantically. "Arrived where?" A sour, sick feeling clawed at my stomach. "What the hell is going on?"

He chuckled, taking a few steps closer, "You're in the kingdom of Nyriathee, where the forest falls away."

Gathering my thoughts, I positioned myself in his line of vision, facing him completely, the lingering pain of my head easing with each breath, "Nyriathee?" It was a strange name for a place. I was sure I'd never heard of it before. I cleared my throat, "And you are?"

He spun the sword once, the hole in the earth growing larger and larger as if we would both fall through it this time, "I don't give my name so quickly to...the human kind."

"You're not making a lot of sense," I scoffed, brushing a patch of dirt off my elbow. "I just wanted to know your name since we're the only two here." The nerves in my chest began to grow into a feeling of annoyance. "So, are you going to tell me who the hell you are?"

"Ah," he nodded, "You're a feisty one...but no, you do not need my name." He reached up, straightening his tilted crown, one hand still steady on the sword. "Know me as leader and King of the Nyriathee Fae and the Court of Starlight."

I was intrigued by his brief introduction. There was a proud, almost arrogant tone to the way he spoke about his so-called power as king of this place.

"Well, King of whatever-the-hell you just said," I shot back, "What was that thing I saw? Before I fell into this...place. I swear something was looking down at me." I scratched the back of my head, "I think it even hissed at me or something."

He paused, "What do you mean you saw *something?*"

My throat burned as I tried to clear it, the grit of dirt scratching it raw, "Before I ended up here, I saw some strange creature. It had this pale, green skin, and its eyes were—"

"Gold," he cut in quietly, "Yellow, perhaps?"

I nodded. "Yes, exactly."

He didn't answer. He only shook his head, as if he already knew the creature I spoke of and my knowledge of it didn't trouble him at all.

I stood silently, letting my eyes drink in the strange and magnificent sight of my surroundings. As he proclaimed himself to be, the king stood rigid and poised, leaning on the sword's pommel as if it were an extension of his own being. He didn't look away. His gaze pressed against my skin like heat from a fire.

He was observing me...studying me. I knew it, yet I tried to stand as though I were unaware. To him, I seemed nothing more than *a human.*

The stillness between us thickened until I couldn't stand it any longer. I wanted to pry deeper, to see what might crack that mask of control he wore so perfectly. "You're not human. Are you?"

His expression didn't shift at first, but his fingers flexed once against the hilt of his sword. "You presume much," he said, his tone smooth, practiced, the arrogance in it almost deliberate. "Humans often mistake what they don't understand for something *else.*"

"That's not an answer."

His eyes flashed, not with anger, but with something colder. It was as if he didn't expect me to challenge him like I had. "No," he admitted finally, voice lowering as if the word itself were dangerous. "It isn't."

The air around him shifted, the way the world changes before a storm. His gaze lingered on me a moment longer before he looked away, almost as if my question had peeled back a layer he wasn't ready to show.

"How do I get back home?" I questioned him, deciding to try a different approach.

"Get back home?" he chuckled, "You can't go home."

Annoyed, not wanting to accept that answer, I questioned him further, "What are you talking about?"

He smirked, "Once you've fallen into Nyriathee, the only way to get back is to *die*."

His words were threatening.

To Die.

I felt a sharp pain in my stomach. I was tired, annoyed, hungry, confused, and still in pain from the fall. I didn't answer him. I didn't need to. He was a strange-looking creature, and I needed nothing more than to return home. I decided I was done here. I was done playing games, listening to his half-ass answers, and feeling my skin crawl from the beads of sweat dripping down my forehead. My best course of action was to run. If I ran, I wasn't sure he could catch me. The outfit he wore looked heavy. He was fit and daringly handsome, but if I stayed here, he could harm me, or worse.

I felt a surge of uncontrollable panic as I pivoted on one foot, turning to leave, but before I could take even three steps, a long, silver blade swung in front of me. I shrieked, peering down at the sword now held at my chest. Flecks of dried blood spattered across it, evidence of its recent use.

"Do not run from me, or you will regret it!" He yelled.

Tiny, pink fairies who must have been watching flew high into the air around us and scurried off to hide. The sight of them was shocking, but only enough to pull my gaze away from the bloody sword for a moment.

"Listen," I spoke angrily, still staring at the blade in front of my chest. "I want to go home. My sister needs me!"

"This *is* your home now." He sneered, "and no one leaves unless I say so."

I turned slowly. His golden eyes had bled into a deep, searing red, filled with rage and hunger.

"Your eyes..." I whispered, "They look like..." I wanted to say *blood*, but the word felt like a lump in my throat.

"Enough!" His shout cracked the air. "I will use this if I have to!"

He lifted the blade, and its cool edge grazed against my throat, a whisper of steel and threat. He pressed it closer, daring me to flinch, "Then kill me." I said, voice low and steady, even as my heart slammed against my ribs.

He laughed, not with humor but with something dark and certain. He drew the sword back with deliberate slowness, "Once you see what's here," he murmured, "you'll never want to leave."

I shook my head, "I-I don't know about that."

His eyes softened, and he placed the sword against the ground once more as if he were never going to kill me from the start. The sword against my throat seemed more of a scare tactic, although the spattered blood made me think otherwise. He reached his hand toward mine, patient yet resolute, "If you want answers, take a walk with me. They're hardly ever found standing still."

I hesitated, unsure of the dangers that awaited me the moment he took hold of my hand.

"Greet no stranger in moonlight," he said with a sly grin. "But if you must, pray it's me who answers."

CHAPTER 3
NYRIATHEE

The strange creature-king stood there, his hand extended, waiting for me to take it. What he said was peculiar, but so wasn't everything else about this place. Butterflies danced in my chest, but the uneasy thoughts fought against them, killing them like a frost in late autumn. Unsure of his true intentions, I gave a soft smile, hoping to be unharmed. I hesitated, reaching for his hand, but decided to take it. The only choices I had were to be killed by him, or take his hand and let him guide me.

His hand was warm against mine, small pieces of hair on the back of it tickling as he intertwined his fingers with mine. I studied it —it looked human enough, yet it still wasn't, compared to any human hand I'd seen. I glanced up at him; he stood around seven feet tall, and he returned my gaze, studying my features with the same quiet curiosity. I felt small next to him, almost insignificant. For a moment, I forgot everything. His eye caught mine, that yellow gleam pulling at me, winding invisible strings until I wasn't sure whose body I stood in anymore.

As we walked, he spoke of the realm of the Nyriathee Fae and the path that led him to kingship. His voice was deep, commanding, and impossible to ignore. He spoke of a place of power and celebration. He claimed it to be called the Court of Starlight. "*My* court." He explained, "A sky that never darkens, though night never ends. Petals that fall from trees with no roots. Music that remembers your name. It's not for humans...*usually*."

He tilted his head."But then... neither are most of the best things."

He explained that he wasn't crowned king by choice, but by birthright. His father had ruled the realm his entire life, and that legacy of rule ran through his blood. There was never a choice to be anything else. He was not allowed to dream of anything other than what he was destined to be.

As he spoke, he shrugged his shoulders, ran his fingers through his dark hair, straightened his tilted crown, and smirked at me. The long, silver sword hung across his back. At times, the moonlight almost blinded me as it caught the sword, streaks of light flashing through the night. I nodded along with him, listening intently to the story of the stranger I had only just met. The stranger who almost took my life within seconds of meeting. He seemed restless yet inviting, sharp-witted, and undeniably fierce. I wondered why he wouldn't tell me his name. Surely, as the king of this place, everyone had to know his name.

"You haven't told me your name," I said, peering up at him.

"I do not share my name with humans," he scoffed, eyes fixed straight ahead.

"Then how am I supposed to know I can trust you?"

He paused, glancing down at our hands—still intertwined. "This," he said, our eyes meeting, "is against the rules."

"Rules? What rules?"

He nodded slowly, shadows flickering across his sharp cheekbones. "Ah, yes," he murmured, "the rules of Nyriathee. The laws." His voice thinned like mist. "They were carved into the marrow of this realm centuries ago, and all who dwell beneath the pale moons have lived...and died by them ever since."

"Everyone but you?"

He paused, and in that silence, as if shocked by what I had said, the forest seemed to hold its breath. His eyes glimmered like liquid starlight as he looked down at me. "The laws," he began, voice a low thrumming beneath my skin, "are as follows:

One. The debt must be balanced.

Two. A name is a blade.

Three. Do not invite the eyes of humans, unless for one's own entertainment."

The last word lingered, curling like smoke.

I swallowed hard, tension coiling between us. "Is that why you won't give me your name?"

"Clever human." A slow smile spread across his lips, sharp and cruel. "A name is a blade. A name is control. And I have no intention of being held by your fragile tongue."

"But you know mine," I whispered, pulse thrumming. "And I never even told you."

"Yes," he jeered softly, leaning closer. "Because I am the King, and you are standing in *my* realm."

Something unseen rippled in the air at his words, bending the light, warping the edges of the trees until they seemed to lean nearer, listening.

My voice came out small. "Number three seems a little... odd."

He tilted his head, the movement birdlike, too quick. "Are you trying to say I invited you here?"

"Well," I stammered, "someone must have?"

"It was not me..." His tone darkened. "Though I did hear your name whispering amongst the trees, calling out to me. Just as I told you before..."

"What's number one all about?" I asked quietly. "What kind of debt?"

He smiled again, and this time it reached his eyes, both terrible and beautiful. "Ah," he said, voice barely above a sigh. "That is the oldest law of all. Every favor, every promise, every stolen breath beneath these stars must be paid."

Silence unfurled between us, deep and thick as the mist curled at our feet. I hadn't noticed until then that he was still holding my hand, his grip light, yet unbreakable, as if the forest itself bound us together.

"And why are you still holding my hand?"

He laughed, low and musical, a sound that made the leaves tremble. "I am the king. I do as I please."

I drew in a long breath, trying to steady my pulse.

"And you," he murmured, eyes gleaming like molten gold, "may run if I let go. You humans are tricky little creatures. You cannot be trusted."

As we walked, hand in hand, the world of Nyriathee came alive in front of me. There were flowers brighter than colors I had ever seen in the human world, and the trees began to hum a soft tune. The wind whispered as it blew through my hair, touching me gently. Tiny faerie-looking creatures lit up the night like fireflies, fluttering around us. This world seemed to come from a dream. It was enchanting. I had never seen anything like it before.

The air was different here. It was warmer, singing with a strange energy that prickled against my skin. The forest around me pulsed with color, the leaves a shade too bright, the shadows a touch too deep. Flowers with glassy petals shimmered in impossible hues, blooming and closing in a rhythm with my breath. The sound of music and wings fluttering drifted lazily on the breeze. Somewhere in the distance, laughter echoed, mischievous, musical, and unsettling all at once.

"What...what is that?" I stammered, clutching his hand nervously.

"That?" He followed my gaze, voice low and guarded, "That is Maulgrove...and his dragon, Tharion."

"Dragon?" I echoed, the word strange on my tongue.

"Yes, dragon." A faint smile ghosted across his lips, but it didn't reach his eyes. "They've roamed these lands for centuries. You may see one now and again...although most keep to the far mountains."

I glanced back at the darkness in the distance, squinting my eyes to try and make sense of what I was hearing—wings flapping, glinting faintly in the starlight. "Are there *more of them?*"

"A few." He admitted. "Not as many as there once were."

"Are they wild?"

"Some," he said softly. "Once, they were bound to Fae kings... partners, guardians. But those days are long gone."

I hesitated, my curiosity outweighing my fear. "Did you ever have one?" I figured that as the king, he should have a dragon of his own.

His expression changed slightly. The faintest shadow passed through his eyes, "Once."

"What happened?" I asked.

He drew in a slow breath, gaze distant, "Not all of us can escape death's powerful grip."

The words were simple and harsh, but they carried an unforgiving ache. I saw something break through his composure. It was a flicker of sorrow, quiet and raw—a weakness, perhaps, though it didn't make him smaller in my eyes. If anything, it made him *real*.

"Oh," I whispered, "I'm sorry."

"Don't be." He said, though the tremor in his tone betrayed him. "She was fierce. Too fierce. Fire and starlight in her veins. I thought nothing could bring her down." His gaze drifted toward the darkness where Maulgrove's dragon vanished. "But there's always something stronger in the end."

I didn't know what to say. I could feel his pain, a strange sadness that almost felt like anger or betrayal. For a moment, the only sound was the faint, haunting melody drifting through the trees.

He broke the silence first. "Maulgrove is...one of the more troublesome faeries. He doesn't always follow my rules. Sometimes, he prefers his own."

"Is he the one playing that music?" I asked quietly.

He nodded. "Yes. Maulgrove is a wicked faerie. Mischief clings to him like a second skin. He delights in bending the rules—tricking, luring, and even harming, if it amuses him."

"So...he's dangerous?"

He nodded. "Dangerous is putting it mildly. He is clever, cunning, and cruel when he wants to be." His gaze lingered on the horizon, where dragonfire flickered faintly. "Especially to humans...and faeries he does not respect."

My grip on his hand tightened. "Well, you could stop him, right?"

A sigh escaped his mouth. "Few can," he admitted, his eyes darkening. "But with me, you are safe. As long as you stay close."

A low mist coiled around the mossy floor, curling around my ankles like curious fingers. I turned slowly, heart pounding, trying to make sense of the place I had fallen into. The trees were taller than any I'd ever seen, their trunks twisted like braids, their canopies glowing faintly with golden light. Other creatures of this strange land rustled in the leaves above as if listening, watching, or both. Their golden eyes peered down from the trees, making my stomach twist in knots.

"By the look on your face, it seems as though you may be enjoying yourself more now," he said, stopping to look at me.

I didn't want to tell him the truth. I was enjoying myself, but I was also terrified. A world had lived below my feet for nineteen years of my life. A world full of creatures, dragons, and things I still haven't seen. I stammered nervously, yet still amazed by what I was looking at, "It's, uh, it's magical."

"Why, thank you." He nodded, "I've made most of this myself."

I took a deep breath, "You? You made all of this?"

"Not all!" He laughed proudly, "Most."

"That's...that's Incredible."

"For centuries, my family has been shaping the beauty of Nyriathee. My father told me he used to scurry away from my grandfather, always bending the rules and practicing little bits of faerie

20

magic whenever he could. His mother tried to teach him some of it, though it wasn't easy for her, since she wasn't actually..."

He let go of my hand, a subtle shift in his presence. "I'm a bit different from most faeries here," he said. "Being royalty comes with...certain advantages. I've picked up a few extra tricks along the way."

"What kind of tricks?" I questioned, watching some faeries fly above his head, one of them blowing a kiss.

Without another word, he lifted his hand and snapped his fingers. The ground shook gently before a patch of small, neon-yellow flowers appeared around us, creating a circle that drew us in closer.

"What would you like?" He asked, smiling at me, his eyes gleaming with flecks of yellow and blue.

It was difficult to tell if he was being genuine or tricking me into believing he was a kind and honest creature. He had nearly taken my life with his own blade, and his actions now were oddly inviting. The mention of dragons that could kill you with one gust of fire didn't help my nerves either. I glanced over at the sword still hanging in its sheath on his back, and panic began to rise in my throat.

"Uh," I said, "To go home."

He looked angry now. "That is *not* a choice."

I felt tears in my eyes. "But why?"

"Because once a human has seen our world, they may use it against us if it is not stripped from their memory. And if it is not, they will never return home."

My mother's voice popped into my head then, replaying the story she told me. *Her friends said she seemed fine, and when one of them turned to her, she was gone. They swore she hadn't screamed, hadn't even made a sound. One moment she was there, the next she wasn't. And the worst part was, she never came back.*

I nodded nervously, "I promise I won't tell anyone what I've seen."

He laughed. "Promises mean nothing to me. Tell me what you want to see, and I can create it for you."

I sucked in a sharp breath, furiously accepting my fate, "Ok, then, Mr. King...I want to see a blue butterfly."

"Just one blue butterfly?" He questioned, "As you wish!"

He snapped his fingers again, and a beautiful, blue butterfly appeared from his fingertips. It took flight, dancing upward into the sky before softly gliding back down, landing on my nose. I reached my hand up, fingers ready to take it off gently, but his hand was already there, removing it and placing it in mine. A strange light sparked where our hands met, small and quick, but unmistakable. I stared down in wonder, still speechless and unable to find the words to describe what I was seeing or how it made me feel.

Although he did not flinch, I wondered if he saw it too.

"It's getting late now," he stated. "Danger will be upon us soon, especially for you."

"What kind of danger?"

"Questions, questions, questions. Always so many questions from your kind."

I shifted uncomfortably.

"Now," He said, "Let me show you a safer place we can go."

Unable to get back home, I agreed, placing my trust in the nameless king. There was no use in trying to run from him; he still bore a giant sword, ready to strike whenever I might try to run.

He led me through a wooded area, still lit with neon flowers and mushrooms of all shapes and sizes. Small creatures scurried along the ground as we walked, each one leaving a trail of sparkles as it disappeared.

"Right down this path." He chirped, glancing over at me.

I nodded, hiding my nerves and expressing slight interest in where he was taking me.

He pulled the sword from his back, and I stumbled away from him, afraid he was going to try to kill me again.

"I'm not going to hurt you..." He claimed, "This will bring us home, well...to my home."

Home.

It was the way he said it, so calmly, inviting in his gentle tone. Home. I had only accidentally been in Nyriathee for a short period, and despite its beauty, I wanted to go home. I wanted to go to *my* home, and I wasn't sure if that was possible anymore. I missed my sister, my parents...I missed the way the hot coffee smelled in the morning, and the way my sister would laugh, jumping on my bed every night just to annoy me. I missed the comfort of Silver Pine Forest. I missed *belonging.*

The nameless king must have sensed the sadness stirring within me, for when I looked at him, his eyes held a strange, mirrored sorrow. "You will be ok here," he said softly.

Then he raised the silver sword high, its blade catching the faint light before he drove it into the earth with a single, fluid motion. The ground erupted in a burst of radiance—brilliant and blinding, as though the very world had caught fire. I stumbled back, throwing up an arm to shield my eyes until the light faded and darkness settled once more.

CHAPTER 4
THE KING'S CASTLE

Before us stood a castle, magnificent in size; it stretched tall into the night sky, the pink light of the stars reflecting off its windows. Its towering spires pierced the sky, laced with ivy. The walls were not made of just stone, but crystal. The doors were carved larger than giants, and lanterns hung, filled with starlight. The balconies rose high above the ground, the pink light of the sky casting a soft glow on the railings, etched with intricate floral designs. Time moved differently here. Slower, like honey dripping from a spoon, and the air swirled with an unfamiliar power that I eagerly wanted to feel.

"This way," he encouraged, "Let us have something to drink."

I sucked in a deep breath and stepped through the doors, weary of what I was leaving behind me in the forest of Nyriathee, and what awaited me here.

We walked into a room, just as magnificent as the rest, and he removed his sword, placing it down on the table in front of him. He glanced over at me quickly, watching me as I watched him lay his sword on the table.

A small rabbit-looking creature ran in through the doors, but stopped to stare at me.

"Hello..." I said, trying to sound friendly.

The creature didn't say anything but turned to the king with wide eyes.

"She is with me," he stated, nodding reassuringly at the creature.

The rabbit-creature glanced back at me quickly and bowed toward him before asking what he wanted to drink.

"Two Emberglow Ciders, please." He insisted, smiling at me for approval.

What he didn't notice was that many of the Nyriathee fae were watching me too. Their eyes glimmered like candleflames in the dark, wide and unblinking, as though a human girl was some rare spectacle.

One figure in particular caught my eye. She was smaller than the rest, no taller than my hand, with the quick movements of a chipmunk. At first I thought that's all she was, until she stilled, turned, and smiled at me. Not the mindless twitch of an animal, but a true smile, sharp and clever, as though she understood something I didn't. Her fur, if it was fur at all, seemed threaded with pale light, markings that shifted when I blinked, forming patterns I couldn't quite hold in my mind.

Her eyes met mine, and for a heartbeat, I felt certain she wanted to speak, to tell me something only I was meant to hear. But then she vanished, scampering into the castle floor with a flicker of silver, leaving me wondering if I had imagined it at all.

The king, still nameless, cleared his throat, and the faerie creatures all seemed to scurry back to where they had been before we interrupted them.

"So," he said, "What do you think?"

"This place is a dream," I stated, shaking my head in amazement.

"A dream?" He laughed, "This is anything but."

The rabbit-creature ran back into the room and placed two drinks down on the table. The liquid inside the container was brown, with golden stars floating throughout it. The container that held the strange liquid was made entirely of crystal, elegant and powerful.

"What's this?" I asked, pointing to the crystal glass in front of me.

"Emberglow cider." He replied, taking a sip, "It's a bit spicy at first, but it has a sweet aftertaste."

I reached for the glass nervously, brought it to my lips, and took a small sip. I coughed, the spices burning as they made their way down my throat.

"Easy there!" He laughed, "This is probably much different than what you're used to, being human and all."

I nodded, trying to be polite, and placed the glass back down on the table. "Just a bit."

As we sat in silence, the nameless king sat with his eyes closed as I scanned the room, taking in the sights. Flowers were growing up the side of the castle walls from the inside, and crystals hung from an enormous chandelier in the hall's center. This place was something I would have read about in fairy tales as a child, not seen in real life.

"Why do you carry that around?" I asked, standing up and reaching over toward the sword, begging for my own sense of protection.

His eyes shot open, and he snatched the sword away immediately, as if warning me not to touch it, "Protection."

"I'm sorry, I didn't mean to—"

He shook his head, "I have only a few guards, but I like to be my own source of protection, and the protection for others who are with me...if they deserve it."

I swallowed hard, remembering the blood on the sword, "Does that mean you've *killed* before?"

He placed the sword back in the sheath on his back, "I do what needs to be done."

"Well," I began, trying to avoid any more uncomfortable conversation, "I'm feeling a bit dizzy."

He nodded, "Must be the cider. It's a bit rough for the first time."

I nodded, leaning into the back of the chair, "I only had a sss..."

He reached over, running his fingers through my hair, "Sleep. Unlike us, humans need their rest."

Before my eyes closed completely, the smile on the king's face appeared genuine. His long fingers in my hair weren't sinister, but gentle. And there it was again. That strange feeling. That spark. I had felt it during our first moments, during our walk. It stung almost like a knife slicing through my heart, but sleep took over before I had time to react.

"Tyvlen...take her to her room." I heard him command before the world went black.

CHAPTER 5
HIDDEN LIBRARY

I awoke suddenly, feeling my body gasping for air. The sound of footsteps scurried throughout the room before fading into the dark. Moonlight pressed through a narrow crack in the window, pale and thin. It was the only light suffocating the gloom. I rubbed my eyes, straining to make sense of the shapes around me.

The last thing I remembered was the king and I seated at an enormous table in a hall of impossible elegance. It felt like a dream, and maybe it was. My skull still throbbed from the fall, a cruel reminder that none of this was imagined.

I was still here. Still in Nyriathee. Alone.

There was a thin blanket, almost like a sheet, laid on top of me, but I pushed it aside and swung my legs over the edge of the bed. My toes brushed against a cold stone floor, and I winced at the chill as I stood. The bottom of my feet were sore after walking through Nyriathee for miles. Every creak of the dark room made me pause, listening, but the silence after those fleeing footsteps was thick and watchful.

I moved slowly, feeling along the walls until my eyes adjusted enough to pick out a doorway. I reached my hand forward feeling for the handle. A cool metal object met my fingers and with a slight push, I heard a click. The door opened and beyond it stretched a narrow corridor, the shadows swallowing the edges. My heart pounded as I crept forward, careful to keep my breathing quiet. I didn't know the time, but by the looks of it, it had to be the middle of the night. I wanted to know where I was and how I had ended up here. I remember the king, the strange drink, and the command, *Tyvlen, bring her to her room,* but after that...nothing.

The hallway opened suddenly into a massive room. Rows upon rows of shelves loomed upward, vanishing into the darkness above, each crammed with leather-bound tomes that smelled of dusk, moss, and something older. It smelled as if the air had been sealed for centuries. Moonlight rippled in from high arched windows, silvering the spines of the old books like diamonds. I took a cautious step inside, nervous, curious, and excited about what I had found.

I stepped forward, unsure of who or what could be watching from the dark. This place was enormous, much bigger than the hall I had been in before. The floorboards were old, as if stolen from an ancient castle, and they creaked gently with each step. There was a small crack in the floor, and something glittered with a golden hue beneath it. I knelt, pressing my fingers to the seam. The old board shifted slightly under the weight of my hand, loose, but not enough to lift. I dug at the edge with my nails, scraping until they ached. Dust caked my fingertips, but I couldn't wedge them deep enough to pry it free. I leaned closer, squinting into the narrow gap. There, just visible in the shadows, was the glint of an ornate corner.

A book. Red. Gilded. Leatherbound.

Something about it pulled at me. Not just curiosity, but something deeper. A weight behind my ribs, like remembering a name I'd forgotten. It must be important. Something in my soul was screaming for me to get my hands on it. To live each page. To learn its secrets. I tried again, this time using the edge of a hairpin, then I found a broken shard of ceramic nearby. The wood resisted, groaning faintly under pressure.

"Come on," I whispered, as if the floor might take pity.

The edge lifted half an inch, but it was just enough. I wedged my fingers in, ignoring the sting as splinters bit into my skin. All it took after that was one strong pull, and the stubborn board came free with a soft, reluctant creak.

"Lost?"

Shit. Shit. Shit. I had been caught, and all that work was for nothing. The book was still hiding underneath the floor. The voice was like ice, cold enough to root me in place. It wasn't the voice of the king. It was eerie and unfamiliar. I snapped the board back into place, ready to play dumb, but knowing I'd return for the hidden book later.

From between two shelves, a tall creature emerged. His skin was a pale, sickly green, stretched tight and thin over sharp cheekbones. His black eyes glittered like wet stone, and his mouth curled in a sneer. Shadows clung to him as if reluctant to let go. It wasn't the king. It wasn't anything or anyone I had seen before.

"I—" My throat caught.

"You are not permitted here," he said, each word precise and venomous. "Return to your chamber. Now."

I swallowed hard, taking a step back.

It moved closer, its tall, unnatural figure towering over me. "I will not repeat myself, human girl."

My throat felt tight, panic surging, and every part of my body told me I had to run. My pulse roared in my ears as I turned and hurried back the way I came, the creature's gaze burning between my shoulder blades until the darkness swallowed me again. Just run. Run. Run. Run. My feet carried me blindly through the corridor, the air growing warmer and heavier until I collided with a hard, solid chest. I flew backwards as if I had been lifted up and thrown. Large hands picked me up, placing me on my feet and steadied me. Gasping for breath, I looked up into the king's sharp, knowing gaze. His dark hair fell loose around his face, catching the dim light, and the corner of his mouth twitched in something between a smirk and a frown.

"And what," he asked slowly, "are you doing, wandering my halls alone in the dead of night?"

The way he said, *dead of night* was terrifying. I gasped until I caught my breath, and then explained everything that had happened. I stammered through the footsteps in the dark room I awoke in, the library, the towering shelves, and the terrifying Fae with thin green skin stretched tight over bones, and eyes that promised nothing good.

The king listened, silent until I finished speaking, and then laughed. It wasn't a warm laugh; it slid under my skin like cold water. He laughed as if I had told him a joke.

"You truly do find trouble without even trying," he said, "But you will not roam my estate without me. Do you understand?"

I hesitated, and his expression sharpened.

"This is my castle," he continued, his voice dropping to a warning purr. "While in Nyriathee, you will do as you are told. No exceptions."

I winced at the sharp steel in his tone, knowing instinctively it wasn't a request. The urge to run back to my room clawed at me, and I took a step to turn away, but his hand shot out, fingers curling around my wrist. I shrieked louder than intended, but he didn't react, nor did he seem to care. He just looked at me, his eyes dark and unreadable, searching for something I couldn't name. The heat of his touch burned into my skin, my pulse quickening beneath his rough grip.

I tore my gaze from his and yanked free, stumbling back before breaking into a run. I didn't stop until I was behind that same door again, in that same dark room, the echo of his stare following me into the gloom.

"That book..." I whispered to myself, "I need that book."

CHAPTER 6
THE KING'S CHALLENGE

The morning light looked different from what I was used to in my world. It had a cyan hue, making the room appear underwater as it reflected against the crystals on the walls. I rubbed my eyes, rolling over sleepily.

Once again, I was alone.

I barely remembered the events from the night before, but my breath tasted of smoke and spice, and the image of the secret book hidden under the floor remained. The drink the king had ordered slipped back into my mind, and I felt my body tense. Did he try to poison me? Was he trying to kill me? Why did he bring me here, back to his castle? What does he even want from me? If I'm *just a human*, as all these creatures so far seem to think, then what kind of importance could I be to this place?

Annoyed, I sat up and swung my legs over the side of the enormous bed. There were no creatures in the room, but I could hear the sound of a breeze blowing through an open window, cool and steady. A small glass, which appeared to be filled with water, was on a table. I stumbled over and took a sip, relief washing over me. The water was deliciously sweet, cool against my tongue. I swallowed the rest in one greedy gulp.

Feeling slightly more awake, I paced the room, the soft thud of my bare feet swallowed by the heavy silence. The walls rose high around me, draped in age with faded tapestries and murals that told stories I couldn't quite decipher. Flowers, painted in rich, wilting colors, climbed the stone like ghosts of a forgotten garden.

The canopy bed I slept in sat tucked into the far corner, its dark wood carved with intricate patterns of vines and stars. A small table occupied the center of the room, its surface polished smooth but scarred by time. Though the space was meant to be inviting, it carried a distinct medieval weight...the kind of beauty that feels both preserved and haunted, as if someone had tried to modernize an ancient ruin without scrubbing away its secrets.

The windows were enormous and arched, framed with heavy drapes the color of crushed wine. Pale light filtered through, washing the room in a dusky glow. I drifted toward one of them, pressing a hand to the cool glass. The air outside shimmered with mist, the fields below stretching endlessly, dotted with strange, dark blooms swaying in the wind.

Then—something moved.

A flicker of motion near the edge of the fields. At first, I thought it was just the wind stirring the grass... until the shape straightened, slow and deliberate, and turned its head toward the castle.

It was the king.

He was standing in the empty field, swinging his sword aggressively. It appeared as though he were fighting off an invisible enemy. He jumped and flipped, stabbing his sword into the ground impressively. Releasing the hilt, the sword remained planted into the ground as if it grew from that very spot. His gaze lifted and locked onto me through the window, as if he sensed my eyes on him. I gasped, hastily closing the curtains, curling myself up onto the floor. My heart thundered in my chest, the sound loud enough to betray me.

Anger began to boil inside me. This place was magnificent, but I refused to be his prisoner. I held my breath wondering if his strange duel outside my window was a warning, or an invitation.

"Are you enjoying yourself?" The king's voice boomed from the doorway.

I jumped in shock, unaware of his presence, "No, yes. I'm-"

He began to smile as he slid a small blade across the floor, grazing my foot.

"Since you enjoy spying as much as you do sneaking around, get outside. Now." He pressed. "It's your turn to show me what you can do with a blade."

"You almost took my foot off with that thing!" I yelped, pulling my feet into my chest.

"Try to run again and I will." He smirked, evil and dark, "No one runs from me. Especially not humans."

I could feel anger bubbling inside me, "I'm not here to be your prisoner! I shouted. "I want to go home!"

"You cannot leave, Liora." He replied, "The trees whispered your name for a reason. I've already told you that."

Tears streamed down my face. "And what am I supposed to do with *that?*" I asked, pointing to the small blade on the floor in front of me.

"Come outside and let's duel." He jeered, his voice cracking with excitement.

"I'm not going to duel with you." I snapped, wiping the tears with the back of my hand. "I don't even really know how to use a blade."

He sucked in a deep breath, "If you fight me and win, I'll let you go wherever it is you're so eager to go. But, if you lose, you stay here with me and learn how to be a true Nyriathee Fae."

"I'll never be one of you." I declared, "And I don't want to be."

He sighed, "No, you won't, but these lands can be dangerous for humans." He took a breath, "You could be hunted for fun, or killed."

He wasn't fazed by my frustration. Instead, he merely cleared his throat, the calm in his voice cutting sharper than any threat.

"Tell me," he said, a ghost of a smile curling at the edge of his mouth, "did you enjoy sneaking around in my library last night?"

I wiped my face with the back of my hand. "I was just looking."

"Looking, huh?" He scoffed, "More like snooping."

I shook my head, my frustration flaring, "It's not my fault you brought me here. I was confused, and it was dark...I couldn't even see."

"Ah, yes," he said with a faint, knowing smirk, "I forgot humans can't see in the dark."

I clenched my jaw. "Who was that, anyway? That thing in the library?"

His mouth twitched into a smile, though his eyes stayed unreadable, "Thing? No. That was Scriptwight."

"Scriptwight?" The name made the hairs on my neck lift. "Who is...Scriptwight?

"A librarian of sorts," he said, glancing away as though the conversation was already over. "He keeps my collection...safe."

"Safe from what?" I pressed.

His gaze flicked back to me. Almost as if trying to warn me. "That's a longer story. One we can discuss later."

I opened my mouth to argue, but he straightened and stepped toward the door, "Come. I'd rather see you holding a blade than pestering me for answers."

Aware I wouldn't win this verbal battle, I rose to my feet and grabbed the small blade. When I looked back up, he had disappeared. The hunger in his eyes terrified me, but a small, treacherous part of me had lingered on the sharp angle of his jaw, the tousled dark hair that fell just above his brow, and the way the candlelight had caught in the amber of his eyes the night before. He was danger wrapped in elegance, a shadow stitched with something magnetic. I hated that I found him attractive, even as every instinct in me screamed to run. If he wanted a challenge, I'd give him a challenge.

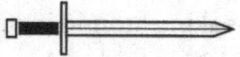

I walked down the corridors of the castle and through the doors. The field was vast and green, with flower gardens, fountains, faeries, and creatures scurrying through the castle grounds. The hot and humid air made my hair strands stick to my face.

He was already sitting in the field outside the window, waiting for me, his sword stuck back in its sheath. "Ah, you made it!" He grinned, "It's time to learn how to be a real Fae, from the true King of Nyriathee himself."

I rolled my eyes, clutching the blade in my hand. The blade I wielded was nothing compared to the monstrous sword he bore. He pulled it out from behind him, the daylight twinkling off its edges.

"Now," He said, "Take a step forward, but don't take your eyes off me."

Nervous, I did as he said.

Excitement rose in his voice, "Good, good! Now, be sure you're holding the blade steady. You don't want it to slip. If it does, it'll rip your hand open, and I'll be able to strike, killing you with one blow."

I nodded, clutching the blade so hard my knuckles turned white, "Anything else?"

He nodded, "One foot in front of the other."

I positioned myself, ready to strike, but a distant sound distracted me, and his sword was at my throat before I had a chance to react.

"I told you to keep your eyes on me." He coached, "You would have been dead."

"What a shame." I whimpered, annoyed by my slight mistake.

"Again." He stated, placing the sword at his side and spinning it in the dirt.

I shook my head, feeling defeated.

His voice was soft, "Liora, you *will* learn. Let us try again."

I sighed, watching him spin his sword around in the dirt as if it were dancing. He looked amused by my defeat, or by the fact that I was embarrassed by it.

"Are humans always this glum?" He joked, "The ones I've seen before were excited to experience a different world."

"I am *not* glum." I snapped, spinning the blade between my fingers.

"Ah, a trick!" He exclaimed, "How impressive!"

The look on his face made me laugh. "It's pretty easy to do."

He was an interesting thing. The only faerie I've truly met, thus far in my time here, and yet, he managed to feel like more than enough. He was unreadable at times, lost in thought, while at other times he seemed proud and unwavering in his power and glory. He lived alone in this enormous castle, shouting demands at the small faerie creatures inside, and yet, despite the emptiness, he seemed happy. Content, even. Like solitude suited him.

"Let's go again," I grunted, ready to prove myself.

He laughed, "As you wish."

I steadied my footing, leaning forward slightly, ready to strike. My eyes were glued to him, my chest rising and falling quickly with each breath. My heart boomed so heavily in my chest that I could feel it in my throat. The air was thick with suspense, time moving so slowly it felt like we were frozen. I was determined to show him how powerful I truly was. How powerful I could be. How powerful I would become.

I stepped forward, swinging the blade swiftly, but his sword caught it mid-air, ripping it from my grip. The small blade flew into the sky as he grabbed me, pulling me to his side. The blade fell fast and stuck into the ground where I once stood.

"Not bad," he admitted, a smirk tugging at the corner of his mouth, "But you were a bit too slow."

Feeling defeated, I shook my head, pushing myself out of his grip and pulling my blade from the ground, "Whatever."

He bowed, "We will practice more soon, but I must go."

"Where are you going?" I questioned as he stuck his sword back into the sheath.

He glanced toward the glowing forest behind him. "Somewhere I am needed."

Time had slipped by as though we had been practicing for hours. It was strange that nightfall had come so quickly.

My stomach groaned with hunger. "Is there anything to eat?"

"Ah, yes, food," he said, "I will have Tyvlen bring bread to your room."

I nodded, a sigh escaping me as I turned around and returned to the castle. I sat on the edge of one of the fountains, blue water bubbling up from the center of a star, shimmering with glitter. I watched as the king moved swiftly across the field, his blade swinging as he ran. Before he left my sight completely, he glanced back at me, a knowing smile spread across his face as if to say, *I know you're watching me.*

CHAPTER 7
MIMSY

Curious and alone, I wanted to know where he went that night. After our training, he slipped away, his hooded cloak covering his face, his golden eyes glowing eagerly. I was nervous without him at the estate. It made me feel more on edge than when he was around. My brain still stirred with the thoughts of dragons. I had met Scriptwight accidentally, but was still unaware of who or what other faeries resided inside.

I shoved the small blade into my dirty boot and walked around the castle property. The stone walls loomed above me, their jagged shadows stretching across the frost-bitten grass. I trailed my fingers along the rough, slime-coated bricks, each patch of cold dampness grounding me in the quiet. The wind carried the scent of pine and something faintly metallic...blood, perhaps, or simply the memory of it. My boots crunched over loose gravel as I circled past the walls, each one reflecting only a sliver of my face. Somewhere inside, strange voices murmured at a pitch I could not make out, yet enough to quicken my steps.

I kept to the edges of the estate where the trees whispered secrets through skeletal branches, their silhouettes twisting against the dying

39

light. The air grew colder here, sharper, as if the castle itself exhaled a warning. Beneath my feet, the ground was soft and damp, dotted with fallen leaves that had long since surrendered their color. The air was thick with the scent of blooming wildflowers and damp earth, but there was something else, too. It was a subtle hum of energy that tingled at the back of my neck and filled the breeze with whispers. Tiny motes of light flickered and danced lazily in the moonbeams, guiding my steps.

Birds with feathers that glimmered like glass flitted between the branches of enormous trees surrounding the grounds, their songs weaving a melody that felt familiar and strange, as if the forest itself were chanting a forgotten spell.

As I rounded the castle's edge, a delicate archway wrapped in vines burst with tiny flowers that seemed to glow from within, their petals pulsing softly with color. Beyond it, the path wound into a grove where light filtered through leaves like shards of gold, and the shadows moved with their own life. They were restless, watchful, waiting.

Even in the darkness, the magic here was palpable, wrapping around me like a silent promise that there were secrets just beneath the surface, waiting for me to find them. But still, I moved forward, drawn by the same restless urge that had followed the king's mysterious departure. What secrets did this place hold? And was I brave enough to uncover them?

A voice broke the silence. "Enjoying the night?"

I jumped, spinning around to face a tiny faerie no bigger than my palm. She had soft, rounded cheeks and the bright, twitching whiskers of a chipmunk, but her eyes gleamed with a cat's sharp, playful intelligence. Her delicate frame was dusted with fine fur that shimmered like morning dew, and her gentle smile radiated a warmth that instantly put me at ease. Despite her small size, there was strength in her presence. Realization hit me fast. She was one of the many faerie creatures I saw in the castle the night when the king had first brought me here.

She smiled gently. "You look familiar. Where did you come from?"

"I... uh," I stammered, trying to find my footing, "The King."

"Ah, yes. The King," she nodded knowingly, "He does love his human pets."

I blinked, caught off guard. "Human pets?"

The words stuck in my throat, a strange mix of confusion and unease swirling inside me. "What does that mean?"

The chipmunk-like creature bowed her tiny head gracefully. "Humans under his care are sometimes more like his playthings than allies." Her amber eyes softened. "But I mean no harm."

I swallowed hard, the forest suddenly feeling a little colder despite the warmth in her smile. "I'm not sure if I'm a pet or something else."

She fluttered her delicate wings, which sparkled faintly in the dappled light filtering through the trees. "Perhaps you're something new. The land shifts with every step taken. Sometimes, it reveals things no one expects."

I looked down at her, so small and fragile, yet somehow endlessly wise. "And what do you see when you look at me?"

Her eyes narrowed thoughtfully, the catlike gleam sharpening. "Potential. And a story yet to be written."

A soft breeze rustled the leaves overhead, carrying with it the faint scent of earth and wildflowers. I felt an odd mixture of hope and uncertainty swirling inside me. "Will I be safe here?"

Her smile deepened, a spark of mischief flickering in her gaze. "*Safe* is a tricky word in this realm. Here in Nyriathee. Here in the Court of Starlight."

"Ok then." I took a shaky breath, "Thank you... for not trying to kill me."

She tilted her head, whiskers twitching. "Killing is not always for me, unless I must. I prefer a more gentle approach."

I stepped forward bending down to her level, curiosity knitting my brow. "Where has the king gone? I thought he would be back here by now."

The creature's eyes darkened, a shadow flickering behind their gleam. "The king does not share his secrets with anyone," she said softly, voice tinged with warning. "Not even with those who walk closest to him."

I swallowed, sensing layers of meaning beneath the words. "But why?"

Her smile twisted slightly, enigmatic. "I will not lie to you. The king is different from us. He's...well, you'll see."

I shook my head, "Different?"

"Be careful what you seek in the shadows of Nyriathee, human girl. Some things are better left unseen."

"Who are you?" I asked as the creature began to turn and walk away.

"I am at your service, miss. You can call me...Mimsy."

Before I had time to say anything else to the faerie, Mimsy, I heard shouting from deeper inside the castle. I froze mid-step. Mimsy tilted her head at me, her expression strangely grim, though she said nothing.

The voices cracked through the stone walls, loud enough to sting my ears.

"You are out of your mind!" one voice roared.

The king's reply was thunderous. *"And you are out of line!"*

Another voice pushed through, frantic and sharp. *"It is not safe— not for you, not for us—to keep a human here. Have you forgotten the last time? Or do you choose to ignore it?"*

My heart stuttered. What did they mean by the *last time?*

The king's tone cut like steel. *"This one is mine. She was brought to me for reasons still unknown. It is I who will decide her fate."*

"That's what you said before!" someone else snapped, rage cracking their voice. *"You promised you could control her, too. And what happened? The girl nearly brought ruin on us all!"*

The chamber erupted, voices overlapping in fury, *"She was no ordinary child—"*

"She vanished into the woods, and the shadow of death followed her—"

"Half the court still bears the scars!"

"Enough!" the king bellowed, the word echoing like a storm breaking. The castle went still. Then his voice dropped lower, venom lacing each syllable. *"I am the king. I will not be questioned. I will do as I please."*

The silence that followed felt heavier than the shouting.

Mimsy's eyes flicked to mine then, dark and knowing, as though she had heard these arguments before, and already knew how they would end.

CHAPTER 8
THE COURT OF STARLIGHT

I had been back in my room for hours, staring at the bread on the table, brought in by the creature named Tyvlen. He dropped it off quickly, bowing before leaving the room. I had heard the king speak his name a few times now, making me think he must be some type of servant.

The king returned late. The forest around the castle was bathed in moonlight, stars, and the strange insects that flickered above like tiny lanterns. I knew he'd already come back long before I saw him. I heard his voice through the castle walls earlier, sharp with argument. Still, I had hoped he would seek me out, if only to prove that last night's words hadn't been empty.

But he didn't.

He'd gone into the forest without a word and returned the same way—silent, distant, as if I were an afterthought. The knowledge stung more than I cared to admit. As much as I hated this place, he was my only source of safety...my only source of strange reality. I had snuck back into my room unseen after meeting Mimsy. She was such an interesting little creature. She seemed to have an understanding of this place that I didn't yet have, but buried beneath my confusion, my soul ached to understand.

Lost in thought, I didn't notice that the king had arrived, as quiet as a mouse. He stood in the doorway to the room, leaning against the frame, staring at me.

"Hi." I said, shifting my eyes toward him.

I wanted to ask about the conversation I'd overheard, to know who he'd quarreled with and why his tone sounded so raw. He wouldn't tell me unless he chose to, and pushing him was my only chance at getting any answers. I wasn't afraid of him, not completely.

"Where have you been?" I asked, nostrils flaring with anger, though my heart beat faster with curiosity.

"I met with the Court of Starlight." He said smoothly.

"Don't lie to me." I snapped.

He laughed softly, the sound echoing like a distant bell.

I stepped closer, narrowing my eyes. "I heard shouting. What happened?"

He met my gaze steadily, unblinking. "It is not of your concern."

"A human like me? A *pet*?"

His eyes widened, "What? Where did you get such a ridiculous thought?"

A cold shiver crawled up my spine, and suddenly, I blurted it out, "I met Mimsy."

His eyes flickered with a spark of something I couldn't name before he masked it with a faint smile. "Mimsy... That troublemaker. What did she say to you?"

I swallowed, recalling her voice's strange mixture of warning and riddles. "She said you make humans your pets."

"I do." He nodded, glancing toward the window before looking back at me.

"Is that what you're planning to do with me?" I asked, my voice barely steady. "Because if you are, it's not going to happen."

He shook his head, "No. That is not my intention."

"No?" I pressed, my voice sharp, searching his face for any sign of truth. "I heard voices—shouting about *the human*. I heard *you* yelling about me too. What's going on?"

His jaw tightened, but his eyes gave nothing away. He didn't answer. The silence between us pressed heavier than the walls of stone.

"Why am I here?" I shouted, the words cracking in my throat. My voice echoed against the vaulted ceiling, raw and desperate. "Tell me! Why bring me here at all if you're not going to explain?"

"Because I asked for you," he said simply.

"You *asked* for me? What does that mean?" I stepped closer, confusion tightening in my chest.

He stood silently, staring at me with his golden eyes. "Most of the time, I am alone."

I scratched my head, trying to understand. "You're not alone. There are plenty of other *things* in the castle. I've seen them."

"That is not what I mean," he said, his tone lowering.

A nervous flutter stirred low in my stomach, delicate and sharp all at once, "Then what do you mean?" The question came out thinner than I intended. I didn't want to know what he had meant, but the curious part of me did.

"Do not worry," the king said, his tone too smooth. "We will speak of it later."

I shook my head, jaw tight. "No. We will speak of it *now*."

His eyes changed. Not dramatically, but enough. The shine in them dulled. Something went still. He looked at me, not as a curiosity, but as a complication. His expression wavered. Annoyance flickered across it, quickly followed by something quieter. Sadness, maybe. Or restraint.

"I was dragged here!" I shouted. "It wasn't *my* choice to come!"

"I understand," he replied coolly. "But you are needed."

"Needed?" My voice rose. "Needed for *what*? I am tired. I am hungry. I've been lied to, ignored, and shoved into corners like some broken thing and you expect me *not* to complain!"

My breath came too fast. My skin felt too tight.

I stomped my foot, childish and unrepentant, and dragged my fingers through my filthy, tangled hair. "I've had enough of this!"

The silence that followed was *too* quiet. The king did not speak. He didn't have to.

From the far side of the room, something stirred. A low hiss, like wind dragging across glass, slipped beneath the floorboards.

Then there was a scent of ash. Damp moss. Rotting flowers. The thought of a dragon crossed my mind quickly, suddenly panicked by the thought.

A presence slid into view, tall and warped like smoke poured into bones. Its skin was bark-pale, cracked in places where veins of silver light pulsed. Eyes like hollow lanterns flickered in its skull, and it moved on too many joints.

"Enough," the king said quietly.

The creature responded to the word as if leashed.

"Take her to her room," the king added, not looking at me anymore. "I would do it myself, but I cannot be bothered with such foolishness. She has forgotten where she is."

The thing stepped forward, and a shiver bolted down my spine.

"Wait—" I choked on my words.

Its long fingers brushed the air around my shoulders and I jerked back.

"Don't touch me!"

But it didn't grab me. It didn't need to.

The air grew heavy, and my knees buckled like the ground had thickened beneath me. I caught myself against a cold marble pillar, gasping. The creature loomed beside me, silent.

"What is that?" I asked, voice rasping. "I thought you didn't have guards?"

The king still didn't look at me.

"That is Veyrix," he said, facing the other direction as if to leave. "He enforces my will."

Veyrix turned its face toward me with a slow, deliberate tilt, then extended one long, clawed hand.

"Come," it rasped, though its mouth never moved.

I could barely breathe.

"You may scream if it helps," the king added, almost gently. "Others usually do. But it will not stop him."

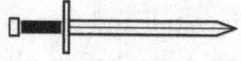

Days and nights passed quickly.

Or maybe not at all.

Time was still unfamiliar to me here. It slipped, coiled, and vanished like smoke. The weather changed just as easily. One moment a warm summer day, and the next, small flecks of snow drifting from a pale sky.

Bread, water, and a red wine-looking drink were brought into my room by Mimsy, the strange little creature with chipmunk features and cat eyes that never lingered too long. She looked at me carefully, like I was fragile or dangerous, but never spoke. She came in quickly, set down what was needed, and vanished before I could ask her anything. I guess Tyvlen wasn't the only servant the king had.

The food began to pile up. Crusts of untouched bread. Cloudy glasses. That red drink, always full, always cold, but never sipped. I barely moved. I felt myself sinking deeper into the cloth of the bed, as if the fabric itself wanted to swallow me. As if I'd become part of the room, just another object left behind. I kept hearing the scrape of Veyrix's claws, the silence in his movements, the way his presence filled the walls even after he'd gone.

The echo of the king's voice played over and over in my head, *"I would do it myself, but I cannot be bothered with such foolishness. She has forgotten where she is."*

Foolish? No. And I certainly hadn't forgotten. Demanding that creature to drag me back here was reminder enough of his careless cruelty.

I was horrified by what the king had done. By how easily he commanded that creature with no emotion, no hesitation. By how little my anger mattered to him. Dragged back here like a prisoner. Locked away as if my will didn't count.

But I am not a prisoner. I will not be. Not for him. Not for anyone.

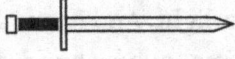

That night, I didn't sleep. The room was too still. The silence pressed against my ears like cloth soaked in water, smothering every thought.

I waited until Mimsy's last visit came and went, until the tray was dropped off, until her tiny shadow flitted back down the corridor. Then I slid from the bed, bare feet silent against the cold floor.

I didn't have a plan. Only a memory. That damn book, still hidden beneath the floorboards in the old library. I needed to find it. It had called to me. It still did. It whispered in the corners of my mind, a golden glint behind my eyes when I blinked.

I cracked the door open and slipped into the corridor. The halls were carved from pale stone and starlight, their surfaces gleaming faintly even without torchlight. The architecture bent in impossible ways. The staircases spiraled upward and downward, and hallways that ended in mirrors or vanished entirely. It looked as though I were living amongst the stars, both beautiful and dangerous.

A strange looking faerie sat in a chair against the wall, his eyes closed as if sleeping, but I knew they didn't sleep. The king had mentioned it before.

Quickly and quietly, I tried retracing the path I had taken when I'd first arrived, guessing at turns, following the patterns on the walls with my hands.

But somewhere along the way... I took a wrong turn.

At first, I thought I'd wandered into a dream, but I couldn't be more wrong.

A great hall opened before me, wider than any ballroom I'd ever seen, its floor shimmering like black glass. The ceiling arched high above in perfect twilight, painted with constellations that *moved*, slow and glimmering like drifting embers.

It was the Court of Starlight. And it was alive.

Faeries—dozens of them, maybe hundreds, were dancing, drinking, and laughing. Their movements were too graceful to be human, their clothing woven from smoke, fireflies, shadow, and silk. Some were tall and willowy, others sharp-edged and aglow with strange patterns etched across their skin. Antlers, wings, tails, or glowing eyes appeared without pattern or logic. They spun in strange, wordless dances. Music filled the air, though I saw no musicians, just sound that seemed to leak from the very bones of the palace.

And the humans.

There were humans there, too; at least I thought they were. Girls with glassy eyes poured wine into goblets that never emptied. Boys in silk masks danced for entertainment, moving with an eerie perfection, almost puppetlike. Some of them were laughing. Others, not. The Fae watched them with amusement, hunger, and indulgence. Like toys. Pets. Or something worse.

And then I saw him. The king.

He sat high above the madness, on a throne carved from obsidian and silver, half-hidden in hanging veils of light. A glass of wine, dark as blood, rested in his hand, untouched for the moment. His eyes, cold and distant, surveyed the crowd like a man watching smoke curl from a fire he'd lit long ago.

His crown shimmered like starlight itself, fluid, ever-changing, never quite solid.

But beside him sat an empty chair. Throne-sized. Carved just the same as his. A place for a queen, maybe, but no one sat there. No one even looked at it.

I couldn't believe what I was seeing. My breath caught and I stepped back, heart pounding.

The Court of Starlight was not still, not empty, not sleeping. It was alive. Starlight poured from the high arches, cascading like silver liquid across the marble floor. Shadows danced where the light touched crystal and glass, forming constellations that shifted with every breath. The air hummed faintly, as though the stars them-selves whispered secrets too ancient for human ears. This was where the king truly ruled—not within the cold stone halls of his castle, not in the shimmering pink forests of Nyriathee, but here, among the endless shimmer and silence of the cosmos made flesh.

And yet, though our time together had been brief, it felt endless. And still, I had never been invited here.

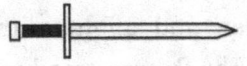

I turned. Mimsy stood behind me, her face tight with surprise.

"I...I...meant to go to the library." I stammered, knowing I'd been caught.

"Library? No." Her voice cut sharp. "You should be in your room!"

I turned back to the enormous glowing hall, my hand braced against the wall. "What is this place?"

"This," she said, lowering her voice, "is the Court of Starlight."

The words hung in the air like a secret I wasn't meant to hear.

"What's happening here?"

"This is where all of Nyriathee comes to celebrate."

"Celebrate what?"

"The stars," she whispered. "And our king who has made them."

My eyes found him again. The king, rising to his feet, his gaze fixed in my direction as though he'd known all along that I was here. It felt almost as if he *sensed* me. The air between us crackled, humming with something unseen. His golden-stitched cloak shimmered like liquid light with every movement and his eyes...those impossible eyes...glowed like twin stars burning in the vast hall.

Mimsy tugged at my foot, urgent. "We should go."

I nodded, though my eyes clung to the vision of him. The chair. The cloak. His eyes. The endless room of light.

"It's all real, isn't it?"

"Yes." Her voice trembled. "Now we must go before you are seen."

I tried not to step on Mimsy as she scurried through the dark halls, leading me back to my room.

"This way," she said, glancing back to make sure I was still following her.

We passed through unlit halls with doors on either side. Some were closed, others open and alight with faeries stirring. Their shadows writhed across the floors, stretching toward us, and the air thickened with whispers that were not meant for human ears.

"Wait," I said, stopping Mimsy in her tracks, "There's something I want to ask you about."

Mimsy peered around the hall before hastily biting and tugging at my pantleg, dragging me toward a shadowed doorway.

"What is it you wish to ask me?" she whispered sharply.

"Well," I hesitated, unsure of how to phrase it without sounding as though I'd been wandering where I shouldn't, "Where is the library?"

Mimsy shook her head at once. "We cannot go there."

"Why?"

"We must get you back to your room before the king discovers you've left without permission."

I gave a half-smile. "He's caught me before."

Mimsy's eyes widened in disbelief. "And you're still alive?"

I laughed softly at that. "I'm not afraid of him."

"You mustn't sneak around, human girl," she hissed. "It is not safe for you."

"But you're here with me now, so technically, I'm not sneaking anywhere. You're showing me the way."

Her sharp-toothed scowl told me she didn't find it amusing. "We must get you back."

"No," I pressed, lowering my voice. "I want to go to the library. There is a book I saw, and I think it—"

"No." Mimsy cut me off, eyes flicking nervously down the dark hall, ears twitching. "Although..."

Excitement leapt inside of me. "Although what?"

Mimsy sighed, the sound like a hiss escaping her teeth. "Scriptwight is not there now... he's with the others in the Court of Starlight. If you truly wish to go, we must go quickly. But not for long."

Her gaze darted upward as if the walls themselves might betray us. "If we are caught, especially by the king, he will punish us. Or worse..." Her voice dropped to a rasp. "He will kill us both."

I nodded, promising her we would be quick. I had to find the book beneath the floor. I had to know why it was there. I had to know what secrets it held.

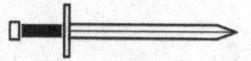

Mimsy squeaked as she tried pushing on the large library door, "It's too heavy," she said.

I nodded, trying to help her, but the weight of the door was unbearable.

"Let me check something." She said before running off into the shadow of the floor.

The sound of footsteps echoed down the hall, "Hurry, Mimsy, I think I hear someone."

The clicking sound of a lock opening caught my attention, "Try it now!" I heard Mimsy yell in a hushed whisper.

I leaned forward and pushed against the door with my whole being. It creaked quietly before opening to the vast library. Excitement fluttered through me. She was willing to help, but curiosity gnawed at the edges of my thoughts. Why?

I pushed the door closed behind me, and Mimsy made her way over to my side, "So, human girl, what is it you're looking for in here?"

"A book," I said, "I saw it in the floorboards."

"A book in the floor?" Mimsy asked, obviously curious, "I've never heard of such a silly thing."

"Yes." I insinuated, "It must be there for a reason."

"Do you think someone was trying to hide it?" She asked.

I shrugged, "That's what I'm here to find out."

We moved together between the towering shelves, our footsteps muffled by the velvet silence. Moonlight filtered through the high glass windows, softer tonight than when I'd first seen it, so faint it barely skimmed the floor. It made it harder to catch the glimmer I was searching for: that subtle shimmer of silver, half-buried in the dark seams of the boards.

"Slow," Mimsy hissed, her claws clicking lightly against the wood. "We'll miss it if we rush."

I crouched low, running my hand across the uneven floorboards. Dust clung to my fingertips, the faint scent of parchment and ink heavy in the air. Every creak beneath my touch echoed too loudly, like a warning.

Then, there it was. A faint gleam, no larger than a coin, winked between the cracks of two warped boards.

"Mimsy," I whispered, excitement threading through my voice, "I see it."

She darted forward, nose twitching as she leaned close. "Silver..." she murmured, her whiskers trembling. "That's not ordinary ink. That's Fae-binding."

I pressed my nails against the board's edge, trying to pry it up, but it wouldn't budge. Mimsy hissed softly, her ears folding back. "Careful! Books sealed in floors are not left there by mistake."

"I don't care," I breathed, pushing harder. "It's here, and I need to know why."

The wood gave with a sharp crack, splintering under my persistence. From the darkness below, the book slid free, its cover gleaming faintly as though it carried its own moonlight. Silver vines curled across the leather surface, forming patterns that seemed to shift when I blinked.

Mimsy squeaked, backing up a step. "Put it back," she whispered urgently. "Whatever that is, it is meant to stay hidden."

But the weight of the book in my hands felt like destiny, as though it had been waiting for me.

"Who is that?" A deep voice boomed, echoing through the shelves.

"Scriptwight is back early. We must go, now!" Mimsy squeaked.

I snapped the board back into place on the floor, ensuring no one would know what we had found.

"Run! Back to your room, quickly!" Mimsy whispered, heading for a small hole in the floor.

I did as she said, the book still clutched in my hand. My heart was pounding, and the vision of the king stained my mind. Even from here, I could feel the weight of his gaze, like ice pressing against my chest.

CHAPTER 9
KING CORVIN

Mimsy had left in a hurry, clearly nerved by whatever we'd uncovered together in the king's old, dusty library. I stayed in my room, the forbidden book resting on my lap, its weight far heavier than it should've been. The cover was worn soft by age, the scent of paper and dust thick in the air.

With trembling fingers, I tried to open it, but the cover wouldn't budge. It was as if the book itself resisted me. I pressed harder, frustration mixing with curiosity, but it refused to yield.

A soft knock against the floor startled me. Mimsy peeked out from a small hole, her wide eyes darting toward the book. "It won't open, will it?" she whispered, stepping inside. "I thought so...that's because it's *Fae binding*. Humans can't open those."

She scurried over to the side of the bed, "I'm not sure I open it for you..." At first, she hesitated, then reached for the book, her fingers trembling slightly. "But I can try."

Before I could reply, she placed her tiny, furry fingertips on the cover and murmured something low and lyrical, the syllables humming in the air like a half-remembered lullaby. The faintest shimmer of light traced beneath her hand. Then—*snap!* The book sprang open, pages fluttering as if exhaling after centuries of silence. A rush of cold air swept through the room, carrying the faint scent of iron and flowers.

She glanced over at me nervously, "Do what you wish...but be careful." With that, she scurried out of the room and back into the dark hole from where she came.

Inside the first few pages, there were sentences, written in spidery, fading ink:

If you're reading this, and you are human, you are in danger. You must be careful. Nyriathee is not a place for humans. The Fae smile sweetly, but every promise hides a price. They live by 3 rules — any debt they make must be balanced. Knowing their true name means you have power over them. And they don't want a human around unless they're under their enchantment for entertainment. Otherwise, you might see too much...know too much. Beware the dragons. They are the ancient sentinels of this realm, bound by no law but their own.

And the King... gods help you if he finds you first. He will belittle you, then charm you, and speak your name like a melody. You will think it's love. You will see the stars in his eyes and feel the world tilt toward him. That is how he ensnares you. He feeds on devotion, weaving it into chains you'll never see until it's too late. I've never seen him use true enchantment magic on a human or Fae, but it could still be possible.

The forest remembers those who wander too deep...and it does not give them back.

I paused. Peering around the room as if I were being watched. What the hell did all of this mean? Who had written this?

"Mimsy!" I called out in a whisper, "Mimsy...come here!"

But she didn't. So I took a breath and read on.

He probably hasn't told you his true name. The Fae hide it well. His name is Corvin, the King of Starlight. Do not be fooled by his silver tongue or the stars of his crown. To love him is to bind your heart to ruin. He will make you regret it, as he has all who came before. Do not trust him. Do not. No matter how much your heart aches for him.

A thin red string fell loose from the spine, tangled and brittle with age. I picked it up carefully, feeling the rough texture against my skin. I flipped through the rest of the pages. They were mostly empty. My fingers traced each sheet, unease curling tighter in my chest.

There were only a few more secrets written throughout the book, but scribbled, almost as if the writer were in a panic.

Red Knotted Thread

Tie it to your door or wear it on your wrist. Each knot wards off the Fae. Should Corvin, the King of Starlight draw near, let the thread stand between you. But beware—thread shields the body, not the heart.

Mirror Glass Charms

Carry a shard of mirror to see through Fae glamour. Their beauty will fade and truth will show. Some don't care how you see them. They'll wear their true face, even as you scream.

Rowan and Thorn

Weave the berries and blackthorn in your hair or wear them around your neck. The Fae cannot use their enchantment on you.

If you have the Sight you've seen things you can't explain. Not everything here has its beauty. You can see through the glamour and that makes you valuable to the Fae.

Each word sank deep, dragging all sense with it. I couldn't think, couldn't breathe. My heart pounded so hard it hurt.

Don't forget his name. Corvin Astravell. One word of his true name and he is yours. But only speak it if you dare. For to do so may summon your ruin.

At the very end, I noticed small, dark stains. They were spots of old blood, scattered across the page like warnings. My stomach turned. Someone had been here before me, someone who had feared the king enough to leave the truth and a part of themselves behind.

I shivered, clutching the red thread closer, the book heavy in my lap. Where the hell would I find rowan and thorn around this place? The Sight? Is that why some things around here weren't as beautiful as others? Do I have _the Sight?_ The warning felt alive, whispering in the quiet room. I knew then that this was not just a story or superstition. The danger was real. This human was scared for their life. The book was bound by a Fae who wanted no human to read it. But why not destroy it?

I flipped to the end of the book and there was a hand drawn image of the king.

King Corvin Astravell. The King of Starlight.

He looked just as he did now, making me think this drawing was done recently. Then again, I didn't know how this world worked, how the Fae aged, or if they even did. I knew they could use magic, but to what extent I wasn't sure. I stared at the sketch, my eyes burning as if mesmerized by it. There was no signature. No trace of the human left behind other than their words, their blood, and the sketch of the king. Who the hell wrote this? I swallowed the panic rising in my throat, feeling it tighten around my chest like chains.

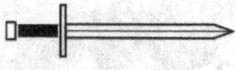

"I find it odd you're in here." A voice boomed as the door to my room slammed open.

I jumped, the book and string scattering to the floor next to the bed. Shit. Thankfully, it fell far enough that he wouldn't be able to see it from where he stood.

His mouth twitched, "What is that?"

"It's uh...it's nothing. Just an old book I was looking at."

The king, who I now knew was named Corvin, stepped into the room, hands clasped behind his back, his sword still hung heavily in its sheath. He looked just as he did when sitting on his throne in the court. Gods, he was beautiful. So annoyingly beautiful. He didn't know I had been there. He couldn't have.

He took a few steps toward me, "You have not been in here all night."

I swallowed, trying to play him at his own game. "Where have I been, then?"

"Not here." He answered flatly.

I nodded, and offered a small, unconvincing smile. "I haven't left this prison, I mean, this *room* in days. You should know since you're ya know, king and all."

He sucked at his teeth before taking a deep breath. "You humans are always lying."

"I'm not lying," I said quickly, keeping my voice soft. "I haven't left this room. I just...I couldn't sleep. Couldn't stop thinking about everything. About home."

He laughed, low and sharp. "But you are. I saw you. In the court."

He leaned down, close to my face, "You were sneaking around without permission again."

I bit my lip, keeping my expression downcast. "That wasn't me. I—I stayed here, I swear. Maybe you saw someone else. I've been dreaming of leaving, of finding a way back. That's all."

He reached out and grabbed my chin, pulling it up to look at him, our eyes meeting, "Stop sneaking around my castle."

I nodded, silent, our noses touching.

He followed my gaze to the fallen book beside the bed, its cover cracked open like a secret gasping for air.

"That book." He said, voice sharp with contempt. "Throw it away. It's nothing but the ramblings of a fool who thought they could bind the truth in ink. Useless."

His hand tightened on my chin. "You would do well to forget you ever touched it."

He backed away slowly as I watched him shove his hand into his pocket and pull out Mimsy. Tears streamed down her face. "You say you're a prisoner here? Well, now there are two of you."

He flung her to the floor and she landed with a harsh thud. Panic surged through me. I ran, scooping her up, checking for injuries.

"I will see you tomorrow, Liora." King Corvin said, his voice like ice, "you're a terrible liar and an even worse swordsman. Let's see if we can at least change that with a blade."

CHAPTER 10
THE SMALL BLADE

Sleep eluded me that night. The stars hung lower than they should, trembling with some omen, perhaps woven by the king's magic and the court's hidden hand. From my window, their light pressed through the lattice like gold bars, striping the floor in uneasy patterns. The castle walls breathed with silence, too thick to offer comfort, and every groan of timber in the rafters echoed like a warning. The air smelled faintly of smoke and berries, reminders that I lived at the heart of the king's dominion, where even the night seemed bound to his will just as the stars were. I curled beneath the covers, yet the weight of the sky, and the weight of his power, kept me awake, listening, waiting.

Mimsy did not want to talk much that night. She lay on my bed, just above my head, her small body curled into the pillow. Her breath came heavy and uneven. Surely, enduring nightmares of the king. What a vile thing, to do such cruelty to one of your own. And it was my fault she had ended up here like this, practically a prisoner in her own realm. She had led me to the library, to the book, but I was the reason she had done so. She wanted to return me to my room, yet I convinced her otherwise. I encouraged her.

The guilt churned in my stomach, hollowing me out until it felt like sickness was filling the space instead. Nausea soon joined in, and I rolled over, gasping softly. I hadn't eaten in days. The crust of bread still sat on the table, hard and stale, waiting. I dragged myself up, broke a piece off, and it cracked in my hands, crumbs scattering across the floor. I glanced over, but Mimsy had not stirred. She remained there, trapped in the clutches of her nightmare. The king's nightmare. King Corvin.

Don't forget his name. **Corvin Astravell.** One word of his true name, and he is yours. But only speak it if you dare. For to do so may summon your ruin.

I wondered what it meant... *he is yours.* And yet... curiosity stirred like fire in my chest, along with a prickling, sharp anger. I wanted to confront him, demand answers about the book. When he said to throw it away, what did he mean? Did he know what was inside it? Did he know the power it held over him? Did he know who had written it, and hidden it so cleverly in the library? Perhaps Scriptwight hadn't been as careful, or as clever as he thought. Or perhaps the king already knew, and I had walked straight into the trap.

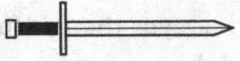

A knock came suddenly the next morning, and Mimsy jumped at the sound.

"Yes?" I said, sitting on the edge of the bed, running my fingers along the blade the king had given me.

A lanky creature opened the door, his eyes flicking first to Mimsy, then back to me. "Human girl, you are being summoned to the court-yard." I thought of the words in the book that talked about *the sight*. I found myself wondering if I could see the king for who he truly was. Could I see any of them as they really were? The first time I saw Scriptwight and Veyrix, they'd looked monstrous like they were straight out of a horror film. And now I couldn't help but wonder if that was their true form, or if the Sight would reveal something even worse.

"Thanks," I sneered, watching the blue-skinned creature give a sad smile at Mimsy before closing the door.

"That's Tyvlen," she said, sighing heavily.

I sighed, apologizing over and over like a broken record.

"No need," she said. "I should have known better."

"You did try to warn me..." My voice trailed off.

"I did," she said with a sniff, "and I was right."

I didn't say anything. I just nodded in agreement, staring at my feet.

"You know, the king can be harsh, but I've seen other sides of him that are...not normal for a true Nyriathee Fae king."

I shot her a look, thinking about what I had read in the book. "What do you mean?"

"He can be...sneaky," she said. Then, after a pause, she added, "But he's not the only one who hides things."

I looked up at her, confused.

Mimsy leaned back, her eyes thoughtful. "He has secrets. They all do. I've seen him hand down easier sentences to Fae who didn't deserve it, you know, things that should have cost them dearly." She frowned, then shook her head as if the memory still stung. "There was one case. It was from a small, miserable creature. Stole from a merchant, but not just any merchant. This one...he poisoned a whole village of forest Fae, but the king gave him only a week in the holding cells. A week! Can you imagine? He walked away like nothing happened. And everyone who suffered... nothing."

I swallowed hard, feeling the weight of her words. "That's...
terrible."

Mimsy shrugged, almost casually. "That's how it works here. You
learn to read between the lines, or you're swallowed whole." She
tilted her head at me. "Speaking of lines, what about that book you
found yesterday? The one in the library?"

"Well..." I started, "It told me his true name and other things..."

Mimsy's eyes widened in shock. "His true name? You...you know
his *true* name?"

I nodded. "I think so...it says it right here." I pointed to the words
on the page, watching her eyes skim over them quickly.

"I...I don't know what to say."

"Do you know who could have written this?" I pressed.

She shook her head. "It must have been someone imprisoned
here before. I don't believe a Fae would ever write something like
this. That would be ridiculous. A death sentence if caught. Do you
understand what knowing his true name means for you?"

I shrugged. "It says I have power over him...oh, and not to fall in
love with him."

Mimsy laughed softly. "I saw that part. What a ridiculous thing
to write."

I nodded. "So...there's also this." I flipped through the pages,
revealing the instructions for the three things I could do to protect
myself.

"A human wrote this," she said, nodding confidently. "No Fae
would ever do something like this."

"Why?" I asked. "Why would they want to help?"

She sighed, a shadow passing over her expression. "Humans are
nothing but a game. Entertainment. Nyriathee is dangerous...you
know that."

I needed to know more. "What do you know about the Sight?" I
asked, pressing her for answers.

"The Sight..." She breathed the words as if they carried weight.
"The Sight is a powerful thing to have. It means you can see through

their glamour. It means a human will see the Fae for who they truly are, even when they've cloaked themselves in beauty."

A chill crawled down my spine. "I think I have that."

Her eyes widened, reflecting something between awe and fear. "You think you have *the Sight?*"

"Yes..." I said cautiously. "When I looked at Scriptwight, I saw what hid beneath. I saw the twisted thing wearing his skin. The same way I saw Veyrix."

She paled. "Then you truly do have it," she whispered. "And that means they know you have it..."

I paused, "But you didn't know?"

"I—" Mimsy stuttered, "I thought you did, but I didn't want to press."

"There's a sketch of him drawn as well, but he still looks the same so that doesn't matter much." I snapped the book closed, "There's this red string that fell out when I was flipping the pages."

Mimsy jumped back, "Oh, no. That is not for me to touch."

"It did say something about protection, but what exactly is it used for?"

"That's for you to protect yourself if you must. Let me see this book."

She took the book from my hand, scanning the pages, rereading the words that explained what the string was for. I nodded, still slightly unsure of what I was supposed to do, but I didn't want to keep asking. I stuck the string back into the book in case I needed it later.

"The king called for you. You should go soon."

I nodded again. "Will you be here when I get back?"

She shrugged. "Technically, this isn't a holding cell. It's just a room..."

"You're right. I'll see you soon?"

Mimsy nodded. "Yes. And tell the king I'm disappointed in his actions—as much as he is in mine."

I smiled. "I'll make sure to tell him that, and use his true name when I do."

"Don't." Mimsy snapped. "That's not a good idea."

"Why?" I asked. "Then he couldn't hurt you, or other faeries, or humans, ever again."

"You would be in charge of the king...of all Nyriathee."

"I hadn't thought of that."

She nodded, "That power is too dangerous for a human."

I sucked in a breath, standing and shoving the blade into my boot. "King Corvin doesn't know the damage he's done to his realm by letting me fall into it. I'm not afraid of him. Train me as a swordsman if he must, but I will show him what true power looks like."

Mimsy didn't reply, but a worried gulp escaped her throat.

"Mimsy...there was blood on the last few pages of the book."

She nodded calmly, "Probably a way to bind the writer's self to the book."

"Hide it when you're done, and I'll be back as soon as I can."

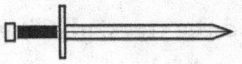

"You are late," King Corvin said, his back still turned to me as he peered out at the forest beyond the courtyard.

"Lost track of time," I replied with a small smirk. "Time doesn't move the same here."

There was a weight to his gaze that made my chest tighten. "Well, we have less time to practice, but we must."

I was ready to play him at his own game. He wanted a challenge?

I'd give him a damn challenge. I moved quickly, quicker than he expected. I slid the blade from my boot, holding it up close to his face, the metal catching the light. His eyes flicked to it, then back to mine.

Before I could react further, Corvin reached out, his hand firm and unyielding, gripping mine. The cold steel pressed against his skin, and his fingers tightened around my wrist, pushing the blade back toward me.

Our eyes locked, and in that moment, the world of Nyriathee, his world, seemed to shrink to nothing but the space between us. The tension was a silent challenge hanging in the quiet courtyard. I could feel the strength in his grip, the authority in his stare, yet there was something unspoken—an intimacy, a spark, a warning all at once.

"You must learn to control yourself," he murmured, his voice low, almost a growl, close enough that I could feel the vibration against my skin. "Or this will end badly for both of us."

I swallowed, my heartbeat thundering in my ears, as the intensity of his gaze held me rooted in place. The blade hovered, not quite threatening, not quite safe, as if it were a test neither of us could afford to fail.

The courtyard was quiet, save for the whisper of the wind through the high stone walls and the distant rustle of the forest beyond. Sunlight dappled the trees, glinting off the hilt of my blade. Under King Corvin's watchful gaze, every movement felt like it carried weight I could not yet measure.

"You stand too rigid, human girl." Corvin said, circling me like a hawk. His boots made no sound, but each step seemed deliberate, calculating. "Your feet. They must move like water. Flexible, flowing, ready to shift at a moment's notice."

I shifted my stance, planting my left foot forward, heel barely touching the ground, right foot angled slightly behind for balance. The ground bit into my boots, but I bent my knees just enough to feel grounded, like a tree ready to sway with the wind.

He crouched slightly, sword in hand, examining my posture.

"Yes... a little more weight in your legs. Keep the center of gravity low. You cannot strike from weakness."

I raised the blade, letting the sunlight catch its steel. It was heavier than it looked, but there was a rhythm to it, a pulse I could learn to feel. Corvin stepped forward, his own blade glinting as he mirrored my stance.

"Grip," he said, taking my hands in his for a moment, adjusting my fingers on the hilt. "Not too tight, or the blade will become an extension of your fear, not your will. Loose enough to feel, strong enough to command."

I nodded, letting him guide my hand. The warmth of his palm lingered longer than necessary, and I felt my pulse spike, but I pushed the thought away. *Focus.*

"Now," he said, stepping back, "strike."

I lunged, aiming for the arc he had demonstrated. The clash of steel rang through the courtyard as his blade met mine. He moved like water, twisting my momentum with a swift parry, forcing me to pivot on my heel. Every time our blades met, sparks—both literal and unspoken—danced between us.

"Faster," he commanded, circling again. "Strike, parry, shift. Feel your weight, feel the blade. Anticipate me, and you will survive."

I gritted my teeth, spinning and thrusting, the tip of my blade grazing his with a sharp clang. He caught my wrist mid-swing, pushing the blade back toward me. Our eyes met, and for a heart-beat, it was no longer training...it was a test, a silent question passing between us.

"Again," he said, releasing me just enough to regain distance. "And this time, do not think. React."

I obeyed, eagerly wanting to strike him with the blade. The next clash was cleaner, my footing surer. The cold of the steel pressed into my palms, the burn of exertion crawling up my arms. Corvin nodded.

Minutes stretched into hours. Each strike, each parry, each step grounded me, taught me something about balance, about pressure, about anticipation. But it also taught me something I had not expected about him. The way his eyes followed every movement, the way his presence demanded attention, the subtle command in his stance that left no room for doubt.

When at last we stepped back, blades lowered, sweat glistening on my forehead, he allowed a small smirk. "You improve quickly, Liora." He said, voice low. "But mastery is not in strength alone. It is in precision, in patience, in knowing when to strike... and when to wait."

I slid the blade back into my boot, feeling both exhausted and electrified. He watched me, unwavering, and I realized that in this courtyard, under his power, I was learning far more than swords-manship.

CHAPTER 11
BURIED TRUTH

The air grew hot and heavy, clinging to my skin. Beads of sweat ran down my face, and I reached up to wipe them away, only to find Corvin's hand already there, brushing gently against my forehead.

"Thanks..." I breathed, my voice shaky.

He gave me a small, tense nod. "Again tomorrow."

"Wait," I urged, panic threading my words. "Please—let Mimsy go. She didn't do anything wrong."

Corvin's eyes narrowed, dark and sharp. "But she did."

"She was only doing what I asked," I said, trying to keep my voice steady.

He sneered. "She's lucky I allowed her to stay here at all."

"What do you mean?" I asked, a chill creeping up my spine.

"She is not a true faerie. Not born entirely of Nyriathee," he said, the words cutting through the humid air like a blade.

I froze. "Huh?"

"She didn't tell you?" His tone was almost mocking, but underneath it was something colder. "I thought you were smarter than that."

73

I shook my head, confusion and dread twisting together. "What is she?"

He leaned closer, his voice dropping low. "She came from human hands. A creature of the human world, shaped into what she is now. She was... a pet when she first arrived here."

My stomach twisted. Mimsy...a *pet?* Not a faerie? And all this time, she had never fully told me the truth...but she didn't have to. She wasn't truly Fae. She was something else entirely. Something that, in her own way, had chosen me just as I had chosen her.

I swallowed hard, the heat pressing down on me, my heartbeat thrumming in my ears. "So she's like me," I whispered, realization dawning with a mix of fear and something like awe.

Corvin's eyes glinted, unreadable, as if he could see every thought running through my mind.

"I guess." He said at last, voice cool but coiled. "But unlike you, she's weaker. The human girl she was with was weak too. And that weakness..." His gaze flicked away for the briefest second, "...is dangerous here."

Why was he telling me this? Was this the start of trust between us, or was this another challenge, another duel, another test?

"The human girl...who is she?"

His jaw tightened. "She was from another time."

"Was..." I echoed, the word tasting wrong on my tongue.

"Yes, was."

The air between us was as heavy as a storm cloud. His tone had slipped, too sharp, too final. I saw it then, the instant realization in his eyes, the smallest crack in his mask. He hadn't meant to say that.

"What do you mean, *was?*"

He looked at me, really looked, as if trying to pull the words back into his throat. The silence stretched until it felt alive, writhing between us. Then he focused a smile that didn't reach his eyes.

"You ask too many questions, Liora."

But it was too late. The damage was done. Whatever truth he tried to bury had already begun to surface. He was learning quickly that the forest brought the wrong human girl here. Or the right one. A human girl who was thirsty for truth. Thirsty to live. And would do whatever it took to stay alive in this strange world.

I decided to press on, "Why doesn't Mimsy look like an animal from my world?"

Corvin nodded, "Because I have made her what she is. She promised me she would stay here with me forever, and in return, I've made her one of mine."

The realization hit me like a ton of bricks. My chest grew impossibly tight, my lungs struggling for air, my heart hammering as if it might tear itself free. Had Mimsy wrote the book? Had Mimsy fell in love with King Corvin? Mimsy was from the human world. She came here *with* a human. Had the human she came here with written the book?

Images I'd held in my mind—every memory, every whispered conversation, every secret smile—flipped upside down. My hands trembled, and a cold sweat prickled my skin. This short amount of time I had been here, in Nyriathee, I had trusted her. I had believed in her. And now... now I wasn't sure I could trust anything, or anyone at all. My breath hitched, a small, unsteady gasp escaping before I could stop it. My thoughts collided, one screaming question after another: *Why didn't she tell me? How could she hide this? Did she even feel what she said to me was real? Who was she, really?*

The hollow ache in my chest spread to my stomach, twisting like a knot of ice and fire. Mimsy had been more than a friend. She had been a bridge between worlds, a secret I had never known I was holding in my short time here. And now that bridge felt like it might shatter beneath my feet.

Slowly, almost against my will, I lifted my gaze, and found Corvin watching me. His eyes, sharp as glass and just as cold, pinned me in place. There was something buried beneath that unreadable surface of his. Something cruelly amused. A smirk tugged at the corner of his mouth, faint but deliberate, as if he knew exactly what that look did to me.

If I had the Sight, he knew it. Of course he knew. He knew I was powerful. For a human. Dangerous even. And he enjoyed it. He craved it. He craved *me*.

Corvin wasn't just training me...he was shaping me, testing how far he could push me before I broke. But he didn't understand yet that I was no fragile human to be molded. He didn't know what he was up against.

A tiny smile ghosted across my lips. It was small, defiant, and deliberate. A dare.

His smirk deepened, a dark glint lighting his gaze. The space between us felt charged, humming with something alive and breathing. Two sharp edges testing each other. Two predators pretending to be patient. The air thickened, pressing against my skin, hot and electric. Every breath felt stolen, every second stretched thin.

And still, neither of us moved.

It was a battle without words, without touch. Just the unbearable tension of two beings who knew the other could destroy them, and found it thrilling.

Then, finally, I looked away. My pulse thundered, but I refused to give him the satisfaction of seeing my hands tremble. The tension didn't break; it merely shifted.

Corvin's voice cut through the air, "Go ask her about it." A lazy smirk still painted on his lips, "I'm sure she'll tell you more half-truths. She is a little liar, after all. Just like the human she came here with."

I sucked in a hot breath, allowing the humid hair to calm me. Corvin may not have realized what he was doing, but he was opening doors for me. I don't mean just teaching me how to wield a blade, or how to protect myself, but how to see his world differently —how strength could be more than muscle, how survival could be more than instinct. He gave me a key to something I hadn't known I was searching for.

He gave me Mimsy.

Corvin walked away, leaving me in the field with unanswered

questions still lingering between us. The humid air pressed against me, heavy as the cloak he wore, but as I turned toward the castle, I hesitated. Something shifted in the dark. It felt like a spider crawling up the back of my neck, the unmistakable sense of being seen, or worse, watched. I froze, eyes darting to the treeline, but the court-yard was empty. Only the branches stirred, whispering secrets I couldn't catch. The night was silent, too silent. High above the tree-line, the faintest shimmer moved against the stars, vast and other-worldly. It looked like smoke, but smoke didn't breathe. Smoke didn't glint with scales. The shape lingered before it vanished, as if swallowed by the darkness itself.

I almost called out—almost demanded whatever it was to reveal itself, but the words lodged in my throat. Finally, I tore my gaze away and forced my feet to move. I told myself it was nothing. A trick of nerves, maybe.

As I walked toward the castle doors, King Corvin stood silent, staring past me as if he had seen it too. His face was pale and rigid. The light from the stars caught his eyes, wet with something that didn't belong to a king.

Grief.

For a long moment, neither of us spoke. His lips parted as if to say something, then closed again. The muscle in his cheek twitched, and he looked away, shoulders bowed under a weight I couldn't name. At that moment, I didn't see a ruler. I saw a man haunted by what he had lost, and perhaps, by what had returned.

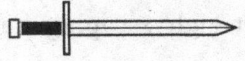

I swung the door to my room open, letting it slam against the wall. Mimsy was nowhere to be found.

"Where are you?" I shouted, my voice raw, the words echoing off the walls.

"Mimsy!" I called again, desperation clawing at my throat. I didn't stop until a tiny squeak reached my ears.

I spun around. There she was, small and trembling in the doorway, her fur slightly ruffled. "Why are you yelling? What happened?"

I shook my head, my hand flying to my boot to draw my blade, pointing it straight at her. "Tell me who the hell you really are. Tell me why if I have the Sight, why can't I see you for what you are?"

Her eyes widened, and a nervous tremor ran through her body. "Close the door," she whispered, voice tight.

"If I close that door, you tell me everything you know," I pressed, every word sharp, heavy with accusation.

She hesitated, biting her lip, then ran a small paw through her fur. Slowly, trembling, she agreed.

She scurried to the bed, her eyes glistening with unshed tears. "What did the king say?"

"You tell me," I sneered, pacing the room, blade still in hand. Every step felt like it rattled the walls themselves.

"Did he tell you that I'm—"

"Not actually a faerie," I cut her off, voice harsh, disbelief and worry bleeding together.

Her ears drooped, and her small shoulders sagged. "Yes... yes, that is true," she admitted, her voice barely above a whisper.

I shook my head, every breath burning. "So...you're from my world? You came here with a human? A girl?"

She nodded, a quiet sigh escaping her. "Yes. Her name was Evelyn."

"*Was?*" I demanded, my voice rising, shaking with disbelief and betrayal. "Where is she?"

"Yes. Was. She died not long before you arrived. I found it odd that the king took such a liking to her. She was... beautiful, yes, but emotional and annoying," she admitted, bracing for my reaction.

I froze, the weight of everything crashing down on me. My chest ached, my hands trembled, and the blade felt suddenly heavier in my grip. Every memory, every moment I'd shared with her, every secret smile now felt like a lie, or at least a half-truth.

My voice cracked as I whispered, "You let me believe you were something you weren't. You're not truly from Nyriathee."

Her eyes filled with tears, glimmering in the harsh light of the room. "I am not," she whispered, almost breaking. "I never pretended to be one of them. I...I just wanted to be near you. You feel like home."

The words hit me harder than I thought they could. My anger wavered, twisting into something heavier, something raw and aching. I wanted to scream, to cry, to collapse all at once. Instead, I sank into the bed, blade falling from my trembling hands, and stared at her, torn between fury, heartbreak, and something like under-standing.

She stepped closer, cautious, tiny paw trembling. "Liora... I didn't mean to hurt you. I never wanted to hurt you..."

And in that moment, I realized I couldn't look away, couldn't push her out of my life, no matter the secrets. Because she had chosen me. And somehow, against everything, I had chosen her too.

"The book..." I said, pulling it from under my pillow. "Who wrote it? You?"

Mimsy shook her head. "Evelyn was always looking for some-thing to write with. She was always trying to get me to sneak off and get things for her. Being so small, it was easier for me to sneak around and steal things she needed."

I didn't say anything; I just listened.

"She had this old book, but I never got a good look at it. I tried once, but she snatched it away before I could. She said it was personal. Something only she could touch."

"So all that work, all that sneaking... it was for this place?"

Mimsy nodded. "She practiced her sword skills with the king almost every day until he found out she was..."

"She was what?"

Mimsy swallowed hard, her eyes dropping. "She told him she loved him."

I blinked. "And...?"

"He laughed. He called her weak. Said she would never be a true swordsman. Would never make a good queen. Said he would never love a human, that it was ridiculous for her to even think it. She ran away. Was never seen again. Tyvlen told me she'd been killed."

I felt a chill run down my spine. "Did Tyvlen say who did it?

Mimsy shook her head, wiping a small tear that ran down her cheek, "I hope it was not the king."

"He wouldn't." I snapped, shaking my head.

She looked up, shaking as if she couldn't believe what she was hearing, "What?"

I shook my head and sank onto the bed. "Corvin wouldn't do that. He might seem harsh, but there's something softer beneath all that armor. You said so yourself. He gave that faerie a lighter sentence than he should have."

Mimsy drew in a sharp breath. "True. But listen to me, Liora...do not, under any circumstance, fall in love with him."

A laugh slipped from my lips. "Fall in love with a king?"

Her eyes narrowed. "He isn't merely *a king*. He is King Corvin. King of Nyriathee. Lord of the Court of Starlight. Handsome, daring, and dangerously seductive. But he will draw you close only to turn the blade when you least expect it. He does not feel as humans do. Whatever kindness you think you see in him, it is only a mask. He cannot truly care for you."

I didn't have the energy to tell Mimsy about the dragon watching me from the field. My mind was focused on the king and the truth about Evelyn. Did Evelyn feel the same heat I felt when looking into King Corvin's eyes? That fire that licked at my chest and left my stomach roiling? Did she feel the dread of the spark, the quiet terror of something wild and uncontainable stirring between them? Did it linger, teasing, pulling, weaving through every glance, every brush of thought until reason trembled? She must have given in. She *had* to have given in—because how could she not? How could any heart resist a fire that seared so completely, leaving nothing but ache and desire in its wake? And if she had... could it have been Corvin who murdered her? That spark I felt. Did Evelyn curse it, or embrace it, as I did, trembling under the weight of knowing what it could mean.

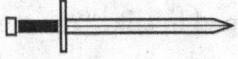

I couldn't resist knowing more about the place I had stumbled into. The land itself felt alive, steeped in magic that whispered through the trees and shimmered across rivers that reflected not just the sky but the unseen. The creatures were strange and wondrous, the faeries both beautiful and terrifying, and all of it consumed me. Every secret I uncovered only left me aching for more, urging me deeper into a world that was never meant for human eyes to see.

The Court of Starlight gathered only at night, when the sky was awash in glittering constellations and the stars seemed to dance above their crystalline hall. Lanterns floated like captured fireflies, painting the marble pillars in gold and indigo light. I told myself I wouldn't return after last time, but the pull was stronger than my promises. So I slipped inside again, unseen, heart pounding as their laughter echoed off vaulted ceilings.

From the shadows, I caught the low hum of conversation. There were noble faeries clustered like jeweled vipers, their voices sharp with disdain. "She is too powerful," one said, swirling wine as if savoring the bitterness of the words.

Another leaned in, eyes flashing like cold steel. "The king must cast her out. His indulgence will undo us all. She can see us for what we truly are."

Their whispers were careless, and I stood frozen in the alcove, each word pressing down like the weight of stone.

"She has the Sight." Another one hissed, "She is more powerful than the last."

A presence stirred behind me. How long had someone been there? Slowly, I turned, and a familiar looking faerie stepped from the shadows, tall, elegant, and sharp as a dagger. I couldn't remember where I had seen him before. His smile was a cruel curve, his gaze a warning wrapped in silk. "You tread where you shouldn't, little human," he murmured, voice honeyed but edged in steel. "Do you know what happened to the last human girl who wandered too close to this court? She nearly ruined everything. Nearly brought us to our knees."

The threat was subtle, but it sank into me like venom, coiling through my veins. I tried to stand tall beneath his gaze, but doubt clawed at me. For the first time, I realized my presence here wasn't just unwelcome...it was dangerous. And if history was to repeat itself, I might already be too entangled to escape.

CHAPTER 12
SECRETS UNDER STARS

knew the king would be waiting for me just before nightfall, but the thought barely anchored me. Something else pulled at me. It felt magnetic. The forest had been calling for days, ever since I'd glimpsed the shape in the sky. I wanted to see what had been watching us.

The air thickened as I crossed the courtyard and stepped beneath the trees. I pulled the rowan berries Mimsy had given me from my pocket and tied them carefully around my neck, ensuring safety against any faeries I met along the way. The scent of moss filled my lungs. The deeper I went, the heavier the quiet became...until it felt like the forest itself was listening. It almost felt like home.

Shadows pressed close, swallowing the fading light. I followed the faint hum beneath the ground as it called to me. Through the mist ahead, the trees opened into a clearing, and I saw it.

The dragon.

Its scales shimmered dark honey in the moonlight—rich and rippling, like molten amber catching fire. Massive wings folded close to its sides, each movement soundless but heavy with grace. Its eyes

83

were molten gold, deep and knowing, their glow reflected in the wet earth.

It didn't roar. It didn't move toward me. It simply *watched*.

There was a strange understanding that passed between us. It was something I couldn't name. It was as if our souls were threaded together somehow. As if we knew the same struggles of this strange world. My fears should have been sharp, but instead, a strange calm bloomed in its place, warm and aching.

Then a voice behind me shattered the silence.

"Liora."

I turned, heart leaping to my throat. King Corvin stood just beyond the edge of the clearing. For once, he didn't look angry. He looked tired. Haunted. His eyes flicked past me to the dragon, and for a moment, something raw passed his face. The dragon shifted slightly, lifting its head to look as if recognizing the sound of his voice.

"Do you have any idea what you've done?" he said quietly, stepping closer. His tone wasn't sharp, but it carried a heaviness.

I swallowed hard, "It's real." I whispered, "You see it too."

He nodded once, slowly. "Yes. And that is why you must never return here."

I searched his face, expecting coldness, but found only sorrow. "Why?"

"Because not everything that watches wishes you harm," he said, "but everything that watches remembers." His eyes lingered on the dragon one last time. "And some memories should stay buried."

He turned as if to leave, then hesitated, glancing back at me. "Come," he said, "You shouldn't be out here alone."

For the first time, it wasn't an order. It was a concern.

I followed him through the trees, neither of us speaking. The forest seemed to exhale behind us, releasing its hold. The dragon did not follow, but its presence stayed somewhere in the space between us. When we stepped back into the open air, the distance between us felt different. For the first time since I'd met him, I didn't see Corvin as my captor or my enemy. He was just a man. A Faerie.

Something was different. The static between us wasn't friendship. Not yet. But the beginning of something that might just become it.

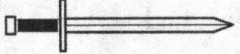

We trained constantly. Time moved differently in Nyriathee, slipping past me in strange, unpredictable rhythms. I couldn't tell how long we'd been at it, only that it was every day. We stayed in the fields until dusk, until Corvin left. I watched the skies for the dragon, but it never came. Each morning, I awoke in bed as if invisible hands had placed me there. Breakfast was served—water, seeded bread, and a maroon jam that tasted faintly of strawberry.

Corvin was changing in ways I hadn't expected...or maybe it was me who was changing. He cracked strange jokes that made no sense but made me laugh. Occasionally, I'd catch him staring at the pink stars, eyes searching, as if the heavens themselves held some secret he was trying to unravel. Slowly, he became more than a stranger. He was gentle, kind, unpredictable, and sometimes, even caring.

When I moved to strike him, he'd always block me, taking a step back just as I stepped forward. My blade would sail into the air above us. He'd pull me close, our faces almost touching, and each time, I'd push him away, heart hammering, afraid of what the spark between us meant. That dangerous, curious spark. I was certain he felt it too.

We let our guards down. Too often, too comfortably, in the open fields beside the castle. I always checked to see if anyone was watching, but Corvin never seemed to worry.

I followed him into the forest more times than I could admit. I was careful, and made sure he didn't know, but the pull to see what he was doing gnawed at me. On sleepless nights, I trailed the faint glimmer of his blade through the dark. He met with creatures unlike himself—some enormous, like living trees, others so tiny they were barely more than sparks of light. The forest bowed to him, and it was clear every being respected their king. I watched to see if he went to see the dragon, but he never had.

The forest of Nyriathee was alive in ways I had never noticed before he touched them. Flowers glowed faintly in the undergrowth, their colors pulsing with the rhythm of crickets' song. Branches bent ever so slightly as he passed, as if eager to brush against him, to remind him they were his. I kept to the shadows, my breath shallow, my heartbeat loud in my ears.

One night, I saw him laughing. Not the wry, cryptic smile he sometimes wore with me, but something freer, unguarded. He crouched beside a creature I recognized—a green being with barklike skin and moss spilling from its shoulders, the same one I'd glimpsed before I fell. It lifted its face to him, and he touched its cheek with reverence, as though it were an old friend.

The forest seemed to lean closer, listening. Firefly faeries wheeled around them in golden rings, and for a fleeting moment I wondered if I had stumbled into a world where he was not training me or testing me, but simply... belonging. The green faerie smiled at him, nodding eagerly to whatever he was saying. Was it his messenger? Another servant, like the ones who haunted his estate? My thoughts flickered to Mimsy—how he had changed her—and I wondered if this faerie had suffered the same fate.

I kept myself pressed to the shadows, slowing my breath, willing my heartbeat to silence. Yet the green faerie saw me. Its eyes darted toward my hiding place again and again, until at last Corvin followed its gaze.

He smiled into the darkness where I crouched behind a great tree veined with glowing blue light. "You can hide if you wish," he called softly, "or you can join us."

I froze. Caught. I had been careful so many times before, but not tonight. Awkwardness prickled over my skin, nerves rooting me to the spot. How had the faerie sensed me? How could it have possibly known I was there?

I pressed my back against the tree, fingers tracing the glowing veins as though I could siphon courage from its light. My throat felt dry. A dozen excuses tangled in my head. I could deny, retreat, pretend I was only lost, but none made it past my lips.

The faerie tilted its head, its moss-hair swaying, eyes reflecting the starlight like a pool too deep to see the bottom, "It is her sir. The girl you asked for."

Corvin waited, calm, as if my spying had been expected all along, as if the forest itself had told him of my presence.

"Why do you watch me?" he asked, not unkindly, but with curiosity. The firefly faeries slowed, their golden light hovering between us.

I thought I could remain hidden, if only I stayed perfectly still. But in an instant, Corvin's hand shot forward. His fingers closed around my wrist—warm, unyielding—and he pulled me from the shadows as though I weighed nothing at all. I stumbled into the circle of light, the firefly faeries scattering upward in a shimmer of gold. He was stronger than I thought.

My breath hitched as his eyes caught mine. Too close. Too knowing. He didn't release me, not right away. Instead, he studied me, as though I were the trespasser here.

"You've followed me before," he said, low, certain. "Haven't you?"

The green faerie's smile widened, moss lips curling as though it already knew the answer.

"I...I..." My throat constricted.

"She hassss," the green faerie hissed, leaning so close its breath chilled my cheek.

I stumbled back. "Please. I only wanted to see what you were doing."

Corvin's hand tightened around my wrist as he pulled me upright. "Liora, there's someone I'd like you to meet."

Brushing dirt from my legs, I turned, and froze at the sight of the faerie I had seen once before.

"This is Esmara."

The green faerie bowed, moss hair tumbling forward. "It isss good to see you again."

So it remembers me.

Corvin's smile didn't reach his eyes. "Ah, yes. Liora mentioned she saw you before she arrived."

Esmara inclined her head, strands of moss sliding across her face. "Yesss... in the Silver Pine Forest. Just as you asked, sir."

"Why were you there?" The question tore from me before I could stop it.

Corvin's brows rose, but he didn't stop me. Instead, he turned to the faerie. "No need to answer."

Annoyance flickered across Esmara's features, as though my voice were an insect buzzing too close. "I was searching for berries. The bright red ones humans keep." She paused, glancing at the king before looking back at me. "Oh, and I was looking for you."

"Strawberries don't grow in the forest." I muttered.

"No." Her glare pinned me where I stood. "No, they don't."

"So you stole them from gardens?"

Esmara's lips curved. It was a half sneer, half smile. "Not gardens. From their homes."

Corvin straightened at that. "Well, Esmara. No more of that."

I tried to smother a laugh, but the sound escaped, "And you were looking for me?"

Her moss-stained hand shot out, seizing my throat. Her grip was damp, earthy, the scent of rotting leaves filling my nose. "Something funny, human? We steal more than berries. We steal humans too. Do you think faeries press wine and gather fruit? No. Humans do it for us. Our good little pets." She hissed, "You think you are here by mistake? No. The king demands and we do as he says..."

Before I could gasp a reply, Corvin's sword gleamed between us, its edge biting into the green of her skin.

Esmara didn't flinch. She didn't need to. Her eyes told me everything: she wanted me dead. And if she'd risked strawberries, what else had she stolen from my world?

Her grip loosened, moss-stained fingers slipping from my throat. Her eyes flicked between me and Corvin. "Be careful, human girl. You are unwanted by many."

Corvin lowered his sword, but Esmara's voice unfurled darker. "The whispers are not quiet. You put all of Nyriathee at risk."

She looked to her king, though her words pierced me. "Humans have already proven themselves dangerous. Untrustworthy. Their lies rot faster than fruit. They are not sweet. They are nothing. They think they can outsmart us, but they are wrong. Nyriathee will be protected from their corruption, no matter who falls to it... even our king."

Her gaze slid back to me. "We will defend this land...even if our king is too blind to see. Blinded by the lies of a human girl."

Corvin stiffened, but stayed silent.

Esmara smiled at Corvin, wicked and knowing. "Your family..." she hissed. "Remember?"

"Enough." Corvin's voice cracked like a whip as he drove his sword into the ground.

I flinched, as if the steel had struck me instead.

"My apologies, king." Esmara's grin only deepened. "But the human girl will not survive here. You know that better than anyone."

Something shifted in me. Her words cut deep, yet a strange thrill stirred beneath the fear. The human girl. Me. Survive or not, she had spoken of me as though I mattered. As though I was part of this world.

I looked at Corvin, my voice trembling. "Are you—"

"We are done here," he snapped, slicing my question short. Rage blazed in his eyes. He tore the blade from the ground and pointed toward the castle. "Go. Liora. Now."

Head bowed, I obeyed, yet every step felt heavy with questions. I could still feel Esmara's grin burning into me, and I couldn't stop myself from slipping behind a nearby tree, heart pounding, to hear the rest.

"Do not speak of my life," Corvin growled. "You are under my rule. You have no right."

"Well," Esmara purred, voice dripping with mockery, "shouldn't she know who you truly are—if you mean to make her your wife?"

The word struck me like lightning. *Wife.* My breath caught, my heart thundering. Corvin... My husband? The idea was wild, terrifying, and yet a strange heat bloomed in me.

"I will banish you to exile, Esmara. Do not test me."

"Exile?" She laughed softly, cruelly. "Tempting. I would enjoy feeding on human souls for eternity."

"Do not speak of my past. I am faerie, as much as any of you. I have made my vow."

The words lodged in my chest like a blade.

Half human.

Corvin—king of Nyriathee—was half human, half faerie.

Shock coursed through me, but beneath it, something else: wonder. Fear and fascination tangled together until I could hardly breathe.

He ruled this world with both bloods at war inside him, yet he stood taller than them all. And though it terrified me, I wanted to know every secret he kept. I wanted to be part of it—part of him. I wondered if Mimsy had known. My mind wandered back to Evelyn, and if she had known it too.

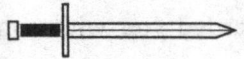

King Corvin and I practiced with the small blade he'd given me. It felt useless in my hand—better suited for swatting insects than true combat. I complained, begged even, to wield his sword instead, but he only ever shook his head.

I longed to speak his true name, to taste the power of it on my tongue, but Mimsy's warning whispered in my mind: *unwise.*

"Esmara..." I began, but he cut me off before I could go further.

"Do not worry," he said softly. "She does not see what I see."

I shifted uneasily. "But she said there are whispers about me... that the faeries of Nyrithee want me dead."

His gaze hardened. "Then they will all die trying."

A smile threatened to break across my face, but I hid it quickly. The king had been nothing but an enemy when we first met. He was cold, cruel, and content to keep me locked away. But something in him had shifted. His threats had turned to warnings, his silence to watchfulness. I could feel it in the way his gaze lingered, in the weight of his words. He wanted to protect me. Perhaps he needed me as much as I needed him.

"Liora..."

"Yes?" I looked up at him.

"There are many things you do not know. You may think you want the truth, but you don't. Nyrithee is a place of twisted games, secrets, and—"

"I'm tired. And I'm hungry," I interrupted, groaning. I feared where his words might lead. "Don't you have anything besides crusty bread and that sour berry wine?"

Corvin's lips curved, as if he knew exactly what I was doing.

"You are far better with the blade than you believe," he said, eyes glinting like onyx in the starlight. "And since you've done so well, perhaps it's time I rewarded you with something finer than stale bread."

Suspicion knotted with curiosity in my chest. "What kind of reward?"

He tilted his head toward the shadowed archway that led deeper into his chambers. "Come. I think I have something you'll like."

Against my better judgment, I followed him. The corridors curved like the insides of a ribcage, lit by pale, floating orbs of light that hummed faintly as we passed. His chamber was cavernous, draped in silks so dark they seemed woven from midnight itself. In the center sat a long table, and upon it a feast that shimmered with a strange, otherworldly glow.

The food was nothing like the hard crusts and sour wine I had expected. Platters of jeweled fruits spilled light as if their skins had been dusted with stars. Loaves of bread steamed, golden and soft, and their scent was so sweet it made my mouth ache. Goblets brimmed with liquid the color of gold and meats glistened with a sheen that looked almost enchanted.

"Faerie food," Corvin said, gesturing for me to sit. "Fit for a king, or a guest who has earned it."

I tried to resist—truly, I did—but the aroma curled into me like a spell. The first bite burst across my tongue, rich and intoxicating, and I didn't stop. I devoured the bread, tore into the meat, drank the jeweled wine until my stomach ached and the room tilted softly around me.

When at last I slumped back against the cushions, dizzy with fullness and warmth, Corvin was already there beside me. He stretched out languidly, his shoulder brushing mine, the air between us heavy with something that felt seductive and dangerous.

"You see?" he murmured, voice low and velvet. "There are sweeter things in my halls than stale bread."

Nervously, I sat up as if lying beside him were some forbidden crime. "I should...go."

"Leaving so soon? You've only just eaten."

I cleared my throat. "I should get back to my room. Rest."

"I'll have Tyvlen bring you more food and drink when you please."

"No, thanks." I shook my head. "I'd rather starve than eat that bread."

"No, no," he chuckled, dark amusement curling through his tone. "I mean this food—the kind you seem to enjoy so much."

"Oh..." I shifted awkwardly. "You don't have to do that, really."

"Well, why not?"

"I...I don't know."

"Liora." He said my name gently. "You are getting better with the small blade. Perhaps I'll allow you to practice with my sword one day, but only if you let me help you first. It is heavier, far less forgiving. Mishandle it, and you'll hurt yourself."

An odd ache stirred in me, something sharp and unwelcome. Mimsy's story returned to me then—of how Evelyn had once trained with him. Was she his pet? His chosen? Is that what I was becoming?

"The girl," I asked suddenly, my voice a blade of its own. "The one who brought Mimsy here. Who was she to you?"

Corvin's eyes gleamed, as though my boldness amused him. "She was a human I thought I might shape into something powerful. But she was not...enough."

"Is that why you killed her?"

Disgust flickered across his face like a passing shadow. "Kill her? No. That was not my hand."

"Then what happened? Do you know?"

He leaned closer, placing his hand against my thigh, his touch cool. "She left in haste, without farewell. She was not strong enough to remain here in my castle."

"I see..." I murmured, caution thinning in my voice.

"You should come to the Court tonight."

I shook my head. "I'm not sure what you mean."

Corvin's smile was sharp, knowing. "But you do. You're not a good liar, Liora."

A chill threaded through me. "Why would I go there? What would they even want with me?"

"They will want what I want," he said simply, as though the matter were already settled. "To see what you are becoming." His eyes glinted like liquid night. "You've already dined at my table. You've already taken in the food of the Fae. You belong more to us than you realize. You are human, and they may not take a liking to you so quickly, but they will in time."

I stiffened. "That doesn't mean I belong at your Court."

Corvin leaned in, so close I felt the whisper of his breath. "It means precisely that. The Court thrives on power, and you carry a spark of it in you. They will taste it the moment you step inside my hall."

Images flickered in my mind, unbidden—faeries draped in silks woven from spider-thread, goblets filled with jeweled wines, eyes watching from shadows, laughter like broken bells. I shivered. "And if I refuse?"

His laughter was soft, but dangerous. "You won't refuse." He rose smoothly, extending a hand. "Come tonight, Liora. Walk beside me, and the Court of Starlight will know you are with me. Or stay behind, and they will still wonder why I keep you hidden away."

The weight of his words pressed against me like iron chains. Some part of me wanted to run, to lock myself in my chamber and never look back. Another part, the reckless part, thrummed at the thought of seeing his world unveiled with invitation from the king himself.

I swallowed hard, unable to form an answer.

Corvin smiled as though I already had.

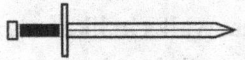

I hadn't been able to stop thinking about the dragon since I saw it watching us practice dueling in the field. Its eyes, ancient and knowing, had followed every movement as though it understood more than it should. Even now, the memory clung to me.

"Mimsy," I began, hesitating, "that dragon I saw...Maulgrove's. The king said they've lived here for centuries, but something about it felt wrong. It was watching us."

Mimsy's face paled a little, "Yes. Maulgrove's dragon." She lowered her voice, glancing toward the door as if someone might overhear. "The king doesn't like to talk about what happened."

"Something happened?" I frowned, "Did the king really have one of his own?"

"Starfire," Mimsy said softly, "She was his bonded. She was beautiful, fierce, a creature of starlight and flame. But Maulgrove's beast killed her."

I blinked. "Killed her? But I thought dragons didnt—"

"They don't," Mimsy cut in. "Not by nature. But Maulgrove used something dark—a wicked magic that twisted his dragon's will. No one knows what kind, only that it left the sky burning for days. The king's never been the same since."

A cold unease ran over me, the image of the dragon's burning eyes flashing again in my mind.

"I'm going to the court tonight. Do you think Maulgrove will be there?"

"You're going to the court? Tonight?" Mimsy shouted, unable to calm herself.

"I guess I am. The king invited me."

"I don't like this." Mimsy said, shaking her head as she paced my room, "Not at all. Maulgrove will probably be there...although he's never been invited. He just walks in like he's still one of us."

"Well, I didn't exactly tell the king I would go. He kind of forced my answer without actually giving one."

"A king will always be a king, bossing everyone around."

A sigh escaped me. "I have to go, right? He personally invited me."

Mimsy shrugged. "Do what you please, but be careful."

I nodded, trying to reassure her I'd be more than careful.

Mimsy scurried off and returned with a small satchel.

"Here," she said, pressing it into my hands. "These will protect you... just like Evelyn wrote."

She pulled out a red string from the book, another necklace made of rowan berries, and gently nudged a shard of mirror glass toward me.

"Remember," she said firmly, "the red string will help once it's tied around your wrist, the berries will shield you from Faerie magic, and the mirror glass shard, well, you don't need it because you can see through their glamor. But take it anyway."

"Ok, thank you." I said, smiling at her.

Mimsy nodded, a small smile curving her lips. "Don't be fooled by their tricks. The Faeries like to play games at the court, especially with humans."

I hesitated before speaking, my voice barely above a whisper. "Mimsy... I met Esmara. She told me something. She said the faeries here don't want me. That they would kill me if they could."

Mimsy's eyes widened, and for a moment she stopped pacing. Her small hands curled into fists. "She's right. They *will* try. You are human, Liora. They will see you as weak, an intruder in their games. In their world. Especially as a friend to the king. Some will hate you just for standing beside him."

Her words pressed heavy on my chest, but they were only an

echo of Esmara's warning, still lingering in the back of my mind like smoke. *Unwanted. Unsafe. Unwelcome.*

Mimsy leaned closer, her gaze sharp. "That's why you must be careful. Do not let them see your fear. And never, ever forget—Esmara may have warned you, but she's not your friend either. She'd just as soon see you gone."

I tried to swallow down the dread rising in my throat, but my fingers betrayed me, clutching tighter at the satchel of charms. "And Corvin? He's not like the others. He's... half human?"

Mimsy's lips pressed thin, but she nodded once. "His mother was human. He doesn't like to talk about it. That's why he's different. Why he's stronger in some ways, weaker in others. Some Fae secretly despise him for it, though they kneel at his feet. It's a secret he doesn't want spoken aloud. I knew you would find out in your own time."

Half human. The thought snared in my mind, tangling with the memory of the way his eyes softened when he looked at me. No wonder he seemed apart from the others—more dangerous, but somehow more real. He looked different than they did. Even with the Sight, part of him still looked human.

My fingers fidgeted with the hem of the dress I had chosen that morning. It was a pale, moss-green gown Mimsy had helped me find from the chest in the corner. It was softer than anything I had worn back home, light as if it had been spun from leaves and grass. Still, it felt like a costume, like I was playing at being someone who belonged here when I knew I didn't.

"Are you really wearing those boots?" Mimsy suddenly asked, her gaze falling to my feet. She pointed to my old, dirt-stained boots—the same ones I'd worn since stumbling into this world.

"Yes, I was planning on it," I muttered, defensive. They were scuffed, worn through at the toes, and carried half the dust of this realm in their seams, but they were mine. Familiar. Safe.

Mimsy rolled her eyes dramatically. "Absolutely not. Here. Wear these."

Before I could protest, she scurried to the chest again and tugged out a pair of sleek, black high-knee boots. They gleamed even in the dim light, the leather supple and untouched by wear. Gorgeous, yes, but they didn't feel like me. They felt like something a faerie might wear to a masquerade, not a girl still trying to hold onto scraps of home.

I hesitated, running my hand along the polished leather. They looked like power disguised as fashion, and I wasn't sure if I was ready to wear either.

"Do not let your guard down, Liora," Mimsy pressed, her tone cutting through my hesitation. "They will test you. They will try to trick you. You cannot fall for it. You must stay alert."

I smoothed the gown against my legs, glancing from my battered boots to the ones waiting before me. Maybe Mimsy was right— maybe it was time to step into something new.

"Okay, okay," I said quickly. "I will."

She squinted her eyes, "And if you see Maulgrove...you know nothing of what we spoke of."

I nodded, "I know nothing."

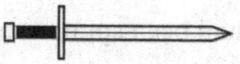

King Corvin arrived shortly after Mimsy helped me get ready for the court. I wasn't sure what to expect, since we hadn't spoken much of it before. What was I really getting myself into? A familiar pit began to form in my stomach.

"Let us have a celebration," he said, his voice smooth.

"A celebration? For what?" I asked, my fingers tightening around the skirts of my gown.

"For the stars."

I managed a half smile and placed my hand in his, though my heart raced. As we stepped through the towering arch of silver vines into the Court of Starlight, King Corvin at my side, I felt dozens of eyes turn toward me at once. The great hall shimmered with starlight caught in crystal lanterns overhead, constellations drifting lazily across the ceiling like living maps. The air hummed with music. It was soft, lilting notes that sounded like silver strings plucked underwater. And yet, beneath the beauty, I felt the weight of their stares. Some faeries' eyes narrowed in quiet fury, others widened with disbelief. Whispers trailed after us like shadows. *A human? Here? With him? Disgusting. She's under his spell...don't you see. But she has the Sight! What an interesting girl.*

Their expressions glinted like shards of glass with anger, jealousy, and hunger. A female faerie draped in moonlight-colored silk sneered, clutching her goblet tighter. Another fae's lips parted in a smile too sharp, as though he imagined what it would be like to strip the flesh from my bone and expose me before them all.

Corvin slipped a little closer, his hand brushing mine for the briefest moment—steadying me, warning me. He, too, felt their gazes, and his frown deepened as if he wished he could shield me from them entirely. Corvin only tightened his hold on my hand, guiding me forward. His face was unreadable now, but his presence silenced the whispers.

I swallowed hard, forcing my chin up, though my stomach twisted. I wasn't sure whether I was stepping into a celebration or a trial.

"Ahhh, the king is here!" a voice shouted, and the court erupted with cheers.

Corvin released my hand and dipped into a bow before the assembled faeries. The room swelled with laughter and wild applause, as though the very air itself vibrated with delight.

"May we feast. May we celebrate the stars, Nyriathee..." He let the words linger, then turned his head toward me, his eyes catching mine like hooks. "And all the things that make our lives dangerously sweet!"

A roar followed—shouts, whistles, and stamping feet. Goblets clattered together as faeries fell upon platters of jeweled fruit and gilded meats. Music quickened; harps and drums wove a frenzied song, pulling bodies into a reckless dance. From the vaulted ceiling above, sparkles drifted like snow, each mote glowing as if the stars themselves had crumbled and come down to revel among them.

Corvin reclined into his throne, the carved wood gleaming like black glass. He smiled at me, watching, always watching, as though the entire spectacle was staged for my reaction. I shifted, uncertain whether I should move closer or retreat to the shadows. Had he known I'd been here before? That I snuck in to watch? Something about the way he looked at me was as if to say, *You already know what to expect.*

"Sit," he commanded lightly, gesturing to the empty throne beside him.

"Oh, no. I'm fine." My voice wavered more than I wished. The throne? Next to him? The thought of it made me sick.

His grin widened. "As you are, then."

He snapped his fingers. Immediately, a small girl scurried up the marble stairs and threw herself into a bow at his feet. She couldn't have been more than seventeen. Her hair was tangled with starlight, her eyes glazed with obedience. Corvin told her to fetch us something to drink, and she looked up at me for a moment—pleading, or perhaps only hollow—before spinning away in a blur of bare feet.

My breath caught.

"Not a prisoner," Corvin said, tilting his head toward me, his smile a slash of white.

The words struck me cold. Every bone in my body told me it was wrong, a violation wrapped in enchantment, yet the weight of his gaze pinned me in silence.

"Don't worry," he added, his tone velvet-soft, too smooth to trust. "She is fine."

If I were going to be his queen...if that truly was his plan, then he had to know this would stop. Using humans for whatever they needed would have to stop. I wouldn't allow it. The music throbbed louder. Faeries clinked goblets and spun with wild abandon, their laughter echoing off the gilded walls. Yet, even as the court roared with joy, I felt the wrongness coil tighter, the shadows lengthen around his throne, and the sweetness of their celebration sour on my tongue.

The girl returned quickly, handing him both glasses of a deep red drink.

"For you, Liora." He said, holding one glass out in my direction.

"Thank you," I said, unsure if I should say anything else.

"This drink won't put you to sleep."

I gave him a fake laugh, "I don't think I could sleep even if I wanted to."

Beyond my chatter with Corvin, I noticed several faeries staring. Their expressions were sharp with anger, and they whispered amongst themselves. I couldn't catch their words, if I'd even be able to understand them, but Corvin didn't seem to notice, or care. Uneasy, I excused myself. Corvin only raised his glass in response, insinuating some type of trust between us. I was strong enough to fend for myself anyways. He knew that. I clutched my drink and slipped through the crowd, searching for Mimsy. She had to be here; there was no way she'd let me come alone.

"Why are you here?" a voice rang out.

I spun, sloshing my drink. Dark drops spattered the floor, pooling like spilled blood.

"I—I'm with the king," I stammered.

"With the king?" One Faerie echoed, laughter spilling from her lips. "Did you hear that? This little human thinks she belongs with the king."

A group of them surrounded me. Their skin the color of pale

moss, hair a vivid, unnatural purple. Their laughter tangled together, cruel and shrill. Some of them were glamoured, but I could see right through it.

"Human girl," one sneered, cutting through the noise. "You will never be *with* him. You are not one of us."

My throat tightened, but I forced the lump down.

"You're nothing but a joke. A game. A pet. He wants you for nothing more than his entertainment."

The words stung, burning hot under my skin. These bitches didn't know me at all. My anger rose before I could stop it, "Piss off."

That only made them laugh harder, the sound echoing like glass shattering.

"Very interessssssssting..."

The mocking stopped. A new voice, deep and rasping, came from the crowd. It was eerie and unnatural as if a demon had entered the room. A faerie stepped forward—massive, his body bristling with fur, but beneath it, his skin glowed a fiery orange like embers under ash. His eyes burned with predatory curiosity.

"Tell me, human girl," he growled. "Did the king invite you here, or did you sneak in, like all the others before you?"

I ignored him, holding my glass tighter.

"You won't speak?" His tone sharpened. "Then I will make you."

He fixed his gaze on me, unblinking, as though waiting for something to happen. The silence stretched. Nothing came. Heat flushed beneath his strange orange skin, his failure written plain across his face.

A smile tugged at my lips. "What was that? Trying to enchant me? You can't. I can see you for who you truly are."

His eyes narrowed, rage simmering. "I'll kill you if I have to, human girl."

"You will not touch her." The king's voice thundered from behind me.

I dropped my glass. Dark liquid pooled across the floor like spilled blood.

"This is pathetic!" the orange faerie shouted. "A human here to enjoy *our* gifts, *our home*? Is it because she has the Sight that you are so enamored by her? Pathetic little rat!"

"I think you are mistaken, Maulgrove," Corvin said, stepping forward, in front of me. "This is *my* home. This is *my* court. These are *my* stars. She is *my* guest."

Oh shit. This is Maulgrove. *The* Maulgrove. The murderer. Both him and his dragon.

Maulgrove faltered, glancing between us as if he were trying to rewrite his wrongs. "My apologies, *King*." His tone slightly sarcastic. "I don't mean to cause any problems."

"It is time for you to leave," Corvin commanded, gesturing toward the gardens.

Maulgrove's glare burned. "But I've just arrived!"

The king was stern, "Go. Now. Or I will make you. You shouldn't have come here."

I couldn't help but glance at the sword slung across Corvin's back. I'd seen him wield it many times before during training, and even now, just the promise of that power made my stomach tighten. He meant every dangerous word.

Maulgrove gave him a nasty look before spitting on the ground in front of me, "You care that much for a human that you would turn on your own kind? Pathetic." He spun toward the exit, "You shouldn't be king. You are not fit for such a role."

Before Corvin could utter a word, a steel blade flashed toward my throat. In the span of a heartbeat, Corvin pulled his sword from its sheath and pressed it against Maulgrove's neck—steady and unflinching. I gasped for breath, watching Maulgrove's blade inch closer and closer to my throat. He seemed eager to anger the king as if it were a game he enjoyed. Though, through his unwavering expression, I saw a small bead of sweat glinting where the edge of Corvin's sword kissed his flesh.

"Leave now!" Corvin roared, a force so powerful it shattered something behind us. I didn't dare move a muscle to see what had broken, for doing so may push Maulgrove's blade directly into my throat. My eyes caught something in the back of the court. It was just beyond the doors. A large figure, all too familiar. Its scales were shimmering in the starlight. The dragon was here and once again, it was watching. Its golden eyes glowed, staring directly at me. A chill ran down my spine, but I didn't dare show it.

Maulgrove exhaled through clenched teeth and lowered the knife. "You will not survive, human girl," he spat. "This place is not meant for humans...even ones who share blood with the Fae." He glared at Corvin before turning around, storming off the way he came.

I exhaled a trembling breath, my pulse still thundering in my chest. Corvin's presence wrapped around me like an unseen shield—one I hadn't known I needed until now, and one I would never forget. He had protected me, standing between danger and death without a second thought.

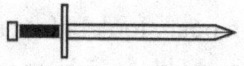

Corvin took me to my room, dragging me by the arm.

"Stop!" I yelled, wrenching it from his grip.

"You were almost killed," he reminded me, his voice low.

"I could have handled it. I have my blade, although it is still far too small..."

He laughed, sharp and amused. "Ridiculous."

"Ridiculous?" I repeated, my voice trembling with more than anger. I raised my blade toward him. "You want to know what's ridiculous? Me, being here—in this insane place with you! You brought me here! You said you asked for me. Whatever that's supposed to mean. You never give me answers. One day you lock me up in this room, the next you let me roam free. You teach me to wield a blade small enough to gut a fish, but never a sword big enough to actually kill someone. If I'm not your pet, not yours to use and entertain...then what am I? Huh? What am I?"

Corvin's expression shifted, eyes darkening. His jaw tightened. For a moment, the anger in my words seemed to strike something in him more than I expected.

"I heard what Esmara said!" I spat. "And Maulgrove insinuated it just now. You are not entirely faerie. You are half—"

Before I could finish, he cut me off, "You will regret your words."

"Regret?" I scoffed, "It will be you who regrets this! When I am dead and you are lying dead beside me! This place is beautiful, yes, but it's obviously incredibly dangerous! Too dangerous for someone like *me*." The words were burning as if set ablaze inside of me, "You want me to be like you? I can't! I'm a human. You're trying to force me into being a faerie! It will not work. It wont!"

"I will not force you to be anything," he murmured, his tone lower now, almost intimate, and my chest thumped in response. He took a breath, peering down at me. "I... I only want to protect you."

I hated how my heart betrayed me, and how a shiver traced my spine beneath the weight of his lingering gaze. When we first met, he had been arrogant and cruel, a man who locked me away only to summon me again for his own amusement. He claimed it was for my protection, and perhaps part of me believed him, but something deeper whispered otherwise. It whispered of secrets he refused to share, of plans that would twist the course of my life more than this cursed place already had.

Without warning, he stepped closer. His hand found my waist, his touch hesitant and possessive. Before I could think, he was guiding me to the bed. My breath faltered, caught somewhere between defiance and surrender.

"Wait—" I started, but he silenced me with a soft brush of his lips against my temple.

I sat beside him, my legs draped over the side of his thigh. My hand moved on its own, fingers finding the hilt of the sword strapped to his back, tracing the cold, perfect lines of metal. His eyes fluttered shut, mirroring mine, and for a breathless moment, the world narrowed to the space between us.

Our mouths hovered inches apart. The air between us was thick, charged, and dangerous. Every inhale drew us closer; every beat of my heart roared in my ears.

"Do you trust me?" he whispered, voice roughened by something between fear and longing.

I swallowed, lost in the pull of him. "I—"

Before I could finish, he stood up, moving past me.

"You're not alone here," he murmured, his voice low, almost a growl. "Every Faerie, every danger...they'll have to get through me first. You are safe, Liora, only as long as I'm between you and Nyriathee. And I don't intend to let anyone hurt you."

"Are you really half human?" I muttered.

He nodded as he left my room quickly. The stillness and shock of his answer lingering in the air.

CHAPTER 13
WHISPERED NAMES

"Liora..." A voice whispered, soft and insistent. "Liora, wake up."

I blinked open my eyes to find Mimsy half sprawled across my face.

"Mimsy," I groaned, pushing her off, "what do you want?"

Her tiny wings buzzed anxiously. "What happened in the court last night? I came in just as the king was shouting, and then I saw him leave with you. Are you alright?"

Rolling onto my side, my eyes still heavy with sleep, I muttered, "I was almost killed, but it's fine."

"Fine?" Mimsy's voice pitched high. "That is not fine! Did you even have your protection with you?"

"Of course I did." I smirked faintly. "Everthing you gave me, and I had the king."

She shot me a flat look. "Ha-ha, very funny. I'm serious, Liora... what really happened?"

With a sigh, I sat up, rubbing my face. "I went looking for you, and a group of purple-haired faeries decided I was their entertainment for the evening." I groaned, leaning back on my elbows, "Maulgrove showed up and threatened to slit my throat."

Mimsy froze. "Did you just say Maulgrove?" Her voice broke slightly. She shook her head, "I knew he'd be there. I *told* them he'd come back. He doesn't care that he's been cast out. He'll always come back."

I nodded slowly. "By the looks of him, that makes a lot of sense. He was...really big. Towering over me like a mountain." I hesitated, the memory sharp as glass, "He held his sword at my throat after the king told him to leave, but Corvin had his at Maulgrove's before I could blink."

Mimsy sat silently, but her fingers twisted together, restless. Her eyes darted to the window as if expecting something monstrous to appear. "Liora, you shouldn't wander off alone," she whispered. "If Maulgrove saw you...he knows your face—"

"He won't come here," I said quickly, though even as I spoke, the words tasted like a lie.

Mimsy's breath trembled, "You don't know what he's capable of. He's not just dangerous. He's obsessed. He's been hunting anything tied to the king since he was banished. You shouldn't have crossed paths with him, not even once."

I tried to steady my tone, "I didn't plan on it." I cleared my throat. "But behind him was..." I paused.

Mimsy's eyes widened. "Was what?" she asked, leaning forward.

"The dragon I saw in the field. The same one I saw in the forest."

The room seemed to shrink around us. Mimsy's lips parted, but no sound came. Her hands clutched the sheet on the bed. "No," she breathed. "If his dragon is with him, then none of us are safe. Not you, not even the king."

I could feel Mimsy's fear. I couldn't tell if the tremor in my chest was from memory, or from the shadow of wings stirring somewhere beyond the walls of the court.

"There's more," she whispered. "Maulgrove's usually not acting alone."

My chest tightened. "Who else would be involved?"

Mimsy hesitated, then swallowed hard. "He's friendly with Tyvlen...and Esmara." Her voice faltered. "You know the names."

I blinked. "Tyvlen," I echoed softly. "I've heard it before..." My thoughts raced, searching for the memory that kept slipping just out of reach. "And Esmara..." I exhaled slowly. "I met her when I was with the king. She's the one that I saw in the forest before I—"

Mimsy gave a short, knowing nod. "I know." Her voice was low, almost regretful. "I hoped it wouldn't come to that—that she wouldn't find you so soon."

I frowned. "You *knew* she'd come for me?"

"Esmara always finds the ones the king wants," Mimsy said, eyes clouded. "And Tyvlen—he's worse. He has close ties to him. He is a servant to the king. He whispers poison into the ears of faeries like Maulgrove. If they're working together..."

"Then what?" I pressed.

"Then it's not just about power anymore," she murmured. "It's about control. And if Esmara's marked you, Liora..." Mimsy's gaze softened with fear. "You're already part of their plan, whether you realize it or not. They hate humans."

A chill spread through me, slow and sinking. I swore I could hear the faint scrape of claws somewhere beyond the walls—like the echo of a dragon remembering my name, remembering my face.

"Maulgrove pressed a sword to my throat." I touched the spot on my neck where the blade had rested, the memory still sharp. "Corvin nearly killed him right there."

Her wings fluttered in a nervous stutter. "That's... that's really something." She sank onto the pillow beside me. "Did he hurt you?"

"Almost." I stretched out my sore arms. "Corvin let him go in the end. I should have stabbed him in the throat when I had the chance."

Mimsy let out a short, nervous laugh. "It'll only get worse if you're not careful."

I frowned. "What? Like the king hearing my name whispered before I—"

Mimsy seized my wrist, her tiny nails digging into my skin. Her eyes were wide with something that looked too much like fear. "Liora... do you realize what that means?"

I shook my head, confused. "That he heard my name? I don't—"

Her grip was surprisingly strong for such a tiny creature. "Liora, if he heard your name, then he *called* for you. Don't you see? No human slips through by accident. Not here. Not to him directly. If your name reached his ears, it's because he wanted it to. He *sent* Esmara for you. She's his spy...his thief. He must know now that she can't be trusted."

"That's not possible. He—he said it was chance. Something that had never happened before."

Mimsy's wings trembled as she leaned closer, whispering like the walls themselves might be listening. "There are no mistakes in Nyriathee. If the king heard your name... it means he wove you into this. He seems to think he needs you."

I stared at her, the weight of her words sinking in. "You're saying... he *summoned me*? Is that why Esmara mentioned me as his..."

"As his what?" She snapped.

"As his wife."

Mimsy's silence was answer enough.

My heart pounded against my ribs. The memory of Corvin's hand on my leg last night, his command for Maulgrove to leave me alone, now rang hollow. He was my protector and captor now blurred together.

Her voice shook when she finally spoke. "Liora, if the king had something to do with your arrival, then you're not here by accident. You're here for a purpose. *His* purpose. And that..." She swallowed hard. "...is far more dangerous than Maulgrove's knife against your throat."

"Well...I..." My words stumbled over themselves. "Next time I see the king I could ask him about it. Maybe, during our next sparring session in the field, I'll bring it up."

Mimsy's wings buzzed uneasily. "Liora, the king is clever. Everything he does is calculated—every gesture, every word. He doesn't do anything without reason. The way he treats you... it doesn't add up. But his actions?" She shook her head. "They tell another story. I think... I think he's falling in love with you."

A sharp laugh burst from me, too loud in the still room. "Falling in love with me? Right. That's ridiculous."

"You said it yourself...Esmara mentioned the word, *wife*." Mimsy shrugged, "If he falls in love with you and you accept this fate, you will be our queen. You will be the *queen of Starlight*."

I shook my head, "This is all getting to be too much."

Mimsy flapped her wings, hovering midair, staring at me with wide, earnest eyes.

"No, listen. Think about it. He heard your name whispered in the trees—the very ones he shaped with his own power. He brought you here, not just into Nyriathee, but into *his* castle, *his* court. His *life*. He's teaching you to fight, to defend yourself, when most faeries would sooner let a human bleed. He's taken you into the Court of Starlight, into his chambers. He's let you eat from his own table." She paused, her wings trembling. "And last night, he nearly killed one of his own kind for you."

"One of his own kind? Maulgrove is an enemy."

Mimsy shook her head, "It doesn't matter. He is still a faerie. If he wanted Maulgrove dead, he would have done that sooner."

Heat crawled up my throat, spreading into my chest like wildfire. My heart pounded so loud I was certain she could hear it. I wanted to deny it, laugh again, push the thought away, but the truth clung to me like cobwebs I couldn't shake.

Mimsy's voice softened, though her eyes still burned with warning. "Do you understand what that means? If he feels something for you... it's not kindness. It's not safety. Love from a king is a shackle, Liora. You wouldn't be his guest. You'd be his possession."

The words struck deep, sharper than Maulgrove's sword at my throat. I opened my mouth, but no answer came. Because even as my skin prickled with dread, a dangerous warmth curled in my chest. It was an echo of the way Corvin's gaze had lingered on me, the way his hand steadied me when the world spun.

I squeezed my eyes shut, whispering, "No. It can't be."

But the silence that followed felt like Mimsy agreed.

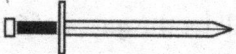

I snuck back to the library that night. The corridors were hollow with silence, and every step I took echoed like a trespass. I was still afraid of Scriptwight. I was afraid of his voice, his authority, the weight of centuries etched in his words, but something gnawed at me: without his knowledge, I would be devoured by whatever shadows ruled this place.

"Hello?" I whispered, the word nearly lost in the dark as I crept into the vast hall.

The scent of dust and candle wax lingered heavily in the air. My fingertips traced the spines of the ancient tomes, rough leather and brittle paper, hoping that the books themselves would answer me, or at least reveal some shift in the currents of power surrounding them.

"What are you doing here?" The voice crackled like lightning splitting the night.

I flinched, spinning toward the sound. Scriptwight emerged from the shadows, his robe sweeping the marble floor like smoke. His hollow eyes gleamed faintly, as though reflecting stars that weren't really there.

"I..." my throat caught, "I think I need your help."

The ceiling above us shimmered, then burst into brilliance, the darkness dissolving into a canopy of a million stars, constellations I didn't recognize burning coldly overhead.

His voice thundered beneath them. "Help? Help a human girl? I think not."

The weight of his words pressed on my chest like stone, but I stepped forward anyway, trembling, refusing to let the fear silence me.

"Please," I begged, my voice cracking, "I need to know what's really going on. The whispers. The Court. The King. The book from the floor. You know more than anyone. Tell me why everything feels like it's unraveling. I feel like I'm in danger."

His form flickered, as though he were both solid and smoke at once. When he spoke again, it was softer, though no less haunting: "The truth is not a gift, girl. It is a burden. Knowledge cuts deeper than any blade, and those who carry it are hunted until their bones turn to dust." He leaned closer, and I could feel the cold of his presence crawling over my skin. "But if you insist on knowing, then understand this: the Court of Starlight will burn if history repeats itself. And you..." His eyes bore into mine, endless voids, "...you walk the same path that lit the fire before."

I swallowed hard, my voice a mere tremor. "What fire? What path?"

Scriptwight's form pulsed with dim light, like a lantern struggling to stay alive in a storm. His words dripped slow, deliberate, each one weighted with centuries of disdain. "There is a faerie," he rasped, "one who despises the King with every breath. His hatred festers like rot, twisting deeper with each passing age. He has always hungered for the throne, though no blood runs in his veins to grant him claim. Ambition without lineage. It is poison, child. Poison that seeps through the Court's cracks."

He drifted closer, the starry illusion above us flickering, "He whispers rebellion to the restless, stirs the hearts of those already wavering in their loyalty. And should history repeat itself, he will light the match that burns this kingdom to ash. His dragon will kill us all."

A chill ran down my spine. I thought I already knew the answer, but I forced myself to ask, "Who is he?"

Scriptwight's lips curved...not into a smile, but into something sharp, something secretive. "His name is spoken only in shadows," he said. "Speak it aloud, and you invite his gaze. But know this: he is nearer than you think. And he has been waiting for someone just like you to stumble into Nyriathee. Into the king's heart."

I gripped the edge of a shelf, my nails digging into the wood. "Why? Why would Maulgrove want me involved?"

Scriptwight's gaze seemed to pierce through me. Slowly, he circled, his presence brushing against me like a cold draft.

"Ah, you already know his name. His hatred for the King runs deeper than envy," Scriptwight said. "Long ago, he coveted more than the throne—he coveted his dragon. He killed her without care, and murdered the girl who once loved the king, all because she did not feel the same about him."

I couldn't believe what I was hearing. Maulgrove killed Evelyn, and Esmara and Tyvlen had something to do with it. They were all in on it. All of them.

"The dragon was only half of the plan. The girl, well, she belonged to no one, yet this faerie desired her, body and soul. His love was not returned, yet his hunger did not fade. He watched her choose the King, watched her give her heart away, and it festered into obsession."

My own heart thudded louder, as though in answer.

"From that moment," Scriptwight continued, his tone sharp, "he vowed to take from the King all that he cherished. If he could not have the girl, then he would see the King suffer, stripped of love, stripped of power. He would kill him if it meant the throne, if it meant vengeance. And even now—though she, and the dragon are long gone—his hatred burns, unquenched."

He leaned closer, the cold of him biting into my skin. "History does not simply repeat itself, child. It is dragged screaming into the present by those who cannot let go of the past."

Scriptwight's gaze lingered, cold and unreadable. "The book you cling to," he murmured, voice like brittle parchment, "already holds fragments of the truth you seek. But the truth is patience. It waits until your eyes are ready to see it."

"The girl... she knew the king's real name."

"She did."

"But why did she write it down?"

"She was bitter," he said softly. "Angry that he did not love her. She claimed the king trapped her, that he wanted nothing more than to use her."

"All because he didn't love her back? That sounds like someone who couldn't handle the truth."

"And so she wrote *the* truth down."

Silence stretched between us. Dust drifted through the shafts of light like restless ghosts.

"His dragon didn't deserve to die," I said at last.

"His dragon died protecting him."

I swallowed hard.

"Human girl..." His voice was low. "I have never seen the king fight his true feelings for someone the way he does for you. You have the Sight...and that makes you dangerous to all of Nyriathee."

My pulse stuttered, "Dangerous?"

"The king's devotion to you is perilous," he said, his eyes glinting like dying embers, "They will hunt you, child. And they will kill anyone who stands in their way."

The words fell like a curse, heavy and certain. Somewhere in the distance, I swore I heard the faint echo of wings, reminding me that in Nyriathee, love was never a blessing. It was always a threat. I blinked, my grip tightening on the memory of that heavy, dust-caked book from below the floor. I finally understood. And it was his words that left a weight in my chest that I carried long after I left the library.

CHAPTER 14
A SWORD

"I need a sword. One like yours." My voice broke the quiet, though King Corvin didn't turn. He stood at the table, broad shoulders tense beneath the shifting candlelight.

"A sword?" He scoffed softly, the sound more bitter than amused. "You are not ready."

I folded my arms. "Then how do you expect me to protect myself against the dangers here?"

Finally, he turned, eyes dark as storm clouds. "You already have a blade. The one I gave you—"

"It's little more than a toy." I cut him off, stepping forward. "Maulgrove nearly killed me last night. If I'd had a real weapon—"

"But he did not kill you, did he?" His tone snapped sharper, as though the words themselves might wound me into silence.

I faltered, heat rising to my face. "No... but he could have. If I'd carried a sword, he wouldn't have dared to challenge me. No one would try."

Corvin shook his head, slow, deliberate. "That is where you are wrong, Liora. The Fae will always test a human, sword or not. Wisdom keeps you alive, not steel."

"I won't hide behind wisdom." I moved closer, the air between us charged, tasting of fire. "I want to protect myself. I want a proper sword. One like yours."

He didn't move as I closed the distance, though his jaw tightened. For a moment, I thought he might push me away, or worse, dismiss me again. Instead, I lifted my hand, daring, and traced the scar along the line of his jaw. His breath caught, so faint I almost missed it.

"What are you afraid of?" I whispered. "That I'll be better than you? Stronger? More powerful?" My fingers lingered, heat sparking where skin met skin. "Are you afraid I might have power over you?"

Corvin's eyes flickered, something dangerous and unguarded breaking through the mask he wore. His hand rose. It was hesitant, conflicted—before curling around my wrist, not to push me away, but to hold me there. He never could have imagined he'd summon a stubborn human girl who would defy all his plans.

"You have no idea," he murmured, voice low, rough. "Power cuts both ways, Liora. And if you carry a blade like mine... you may find it's not the faeries here you need protecting from."

My heart hammered, remembering the dragon. I should have stepped back, but instead I leaned closer, caught in the pull of him— the danger, the promise, the mystery.

"Then teach me," I breathed. "If you're so afraid of what I might become, then make certain I become it on your terms."

The king leaned in close, his lips barely brushing mine. I gasped, the sound swallowed in the closeness of him, in the warmth of his breath ghosting across my mouth. His hand settled on my hips, firm and unyielding, pulling me against him as though he dared me to resist.

Every nerve in my body caught fire. I knew I should step away— that this was dangerous, reckless, but his nearness unraveled every thought, every shred of caution I'd clung to.

"Careful, human girl," he whispered, his voice rough against my skin. "One taste, and neither of us will stop."

My fingers curled into the fabric of his cloak, trembling not with fear but with something intoxicating. I tilted my chin up, so close our lips almost met. I pressed my palm against his chest and stepped back.

He stilled, surprise flickering across his face.

I tilted my head, letting a slow, knowing smile curve my lips. "Tempting," I said, my voice smooth as silk. "But what I really want..." I let my eyes trail over the sword at his back, then back up to meet his gaze. "...is a sword of my own."

His jaw tightened, the fire in his eyes shifting, but I only smirked wider. I turned on my heel, hips swaying just enough to remind him of the power I held, and left him standing there—wanting, frustrated, and very much alone.

CHAPTER 15
MIDNIGHT ATTACK

"You should have seen the way he stood there all tense and confused as I left. It was perfect!" I laughed, spinning across the room while Mimsy watched.

"I knew I was right," she said, a confident smile tugging at her lips.

"I still want my own sword." I drew the small blade from my boot, holding it up with exaggerated drama. "This thing wouldn't do much damage against anything serious."

Mimsy sighed. "I'm not sure why Evelyn confessed her love to him."

I froze mid-spin, frowning at her.

She looked up at me, "I'm confused. Really. He said he couldn't love a human, yet he seems enamored with you."

I shrugged. "I'm not sure why. I've been nothing but a thorn in his side since I got here."

A small laugh escaped her. "But you're a thorn with a rose attached. Evelyn was just the flower. You have a power he desires. He enjoys a challenge."

I smirked, "He thinks he has power over me, but I'll show him true power."

Mimsy lifted a furry eyebrow, unimpressed. "Oh, Liora, that tone never ends well."

"Please," I said, spinning in a slow circle before collapsing onto the bed. "I will reel him in just to cast him out. You never want a man to know he's got you."

Mimsy folded her arms, her wings fluttering with agitation. "You talk like you're playing a game, but you forget...he's the king. And kings don't lose."

I propped myself up on my elbows, grin still tugging at my lips, "Then maybe he's never played against someone like me."

"Liora..." Mimsy's voice softened. "You're treading on dangerous ground. The court whispered already. Some say the king's losing his grip because of you. If they believe that's true, they'll come for you both."

My smirk faltered, though I tried to hide it, "Let them try."

"You don't understand." Mimsy stepped closer, lowering her voice. "This isn't a battle of affection or pride...it's survival. If you push him too far, he won't be the one who pays for it all. *You will.*"

I turned to face the ceiling above, forcing a laugh I didn't quite feel. "I've already survived worse."

Mimsy sighed, wings dimming with the light. "I hope that's still the truth when the game ends."

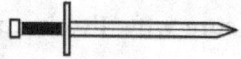

I woke to the sound of metal scraping against wood, a sharp, grating noise that made my blood run cold. My heart slammed against my ribs, and every nerve in my body screamed that something was wrong. Shadows danced across the room in the pale moonlight, but one of them moved too quickly, too deliberately to be harmless. I thought of Maulgrove, his stature too large and wide for it to be him.

"Mimsy..." I whispered, and my gaze darted to the corner. She froze, then bolted toward the hole in the wall, disappearing with a soft squeak. Shit. My stomach knotted, but there was no time to follow. I gripped the hilt of my blade, feeling its familiar weight grounding me.

"Come and get me." I sneered, "It will be you who regrets it."

The room fell into a brittle silence. I squinted into the dark, trying to pin the movement with my eyes.

"Silly girl," they hissed. "You will die."

The intruder lunged. Instinct took over; fear sharpened into a single, clean focus. I swung and the blade sang through the air. I teetered on the bed, feet slipping on linen, heart hammering. "Coward!" I shouted, my fingers white from gripping the blade.

"After we kill you, we will kill the king." The voice spat the words like a curse. A shadow flickered across the far wall.

I lost control of my swing, wild and raw, until the steel found flesh with a wet, sick thunk. Whoever it was yelped and stumbled back, a bright, animal sound that pierced my ears. Blood flecked the moonlight on my blade. I leapt down, knees unsteady, the metal trembling in my hand. "Who are you?" I demanded, voice sharp, breath ragged.

A hiss slid across the room, both cold and venomous. "The king will fall. Nyriathee will fall. The dragons whisper the fate of us all."

My grip tightened until my knuckles ached. "Who are you?" I said it again, harder this time. Fear and fury braided in my throat.

They glided closer. Moonlight carved its face into knives—angular, cruel, eyes like coals. Then it smiled, slow and certain, and for the first time I saw the name behind the threat.

"It's Tyvlen," he said, as if introducing himself to an old friend. "Maulgrove sends his apologies. Esmara sends her regards."

Something cold uncoiled in my chest. The room narrowed to his voice and the wet gleam of my blade. I planted my feet, refusing to let the tremor in my limbs show. "You picked the wrong human," I snapped, though the sound was thin. Behind him, the moon-shadow of wings—too large, too patient—stirred like a promise.

My heart lurched, but I forced my feet to hold. "What the hell do you want?" I spat, thrusting the blade toward him.

His lips curled into something between a smirk and a snarl. "What I want is irrelevant. What *you* are... that is everything. You will die, girl—by my hand, or another's. Fate is already sharpening the knife."

I swallowed hard, forcing steel into my words. "I don't care what fate says. I'll protect myself, and the king, no matter the cost."

My words made Tyvlen's smile widened, predatory. "Ah. The king's hound bares her teeth. How touching." He stepped closer, his voice dropping to a whisper that slithered into my bones. "You chain yourself to him, when all that binds you is weakness. I offer you something greater. Freedom. Power. A life beyond his shadow."

I lifted my chin, though my chest ached with fear. "I won't betray him."

"You will," Tyvlen murmured, eyes glinting like flint. "When you feel death's breath on your neck, when your blade alone cannot hold the tide, you'll know. Kill the king, and the leash falls away. Refuse... and you will watch him fall, and die screaming beside him."

My blade quivered in my hand. For the first time, I felt not just fear, but the heavy, horrible weight of the choice he pressed against me. He let the silence stretch, savoring it, then his smile turned even more cruel.

Without another word he moved to the window. The glass threw his silhouette in fractured light as he shoved it open and vaulted out with the effortless grace of something that did not belong to this world. He left a smear of dark crimson on the sill as if the night itself had bled.

I sank to my knees, legs finally giving out beneath me. My hands shook so hard the blade rattled. The room was quiet now except for Mimsy's tentative whine from where she peered out of her hiding place. Relief, though thin and trembling, washed through me. I had done it. I had protected her. I protected myself. For tonight, at least, we had survived.

But as I pressed my palms to my knees and tried to slow my breath, the echo of his words wound around my spine. *Kill the king. Watch him die.* The choice it set before me gleamed like a promise and a threat both, and I knew whatever came next would not be undone by a single night's victory.

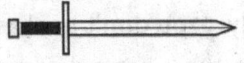

CORVIN BURST into the room moments later, his breathing ragged, heavier than I'd ever heard before. "What happened?" he barked, eyes wild as he drew his sword, scanning the shadows.

"I—I was—"

"She was attacked!" Mimsy shrieked, crawling out from the small hole where she'd been hiding. Her wings trembled, her eyes wide with panic.

"He went out the window," I gasped, trying to still my trembling hands.

Corvin spun toward the open pane, the night wind howling through it. He leaned out, shouting words I couldn't make out—

sharp, commanding, filled with fury. His voice carried the weight of warning. The name *Tyvlen* seared through my mind like fire.

Veyrix stormed in seconds later, his massive frame blocking the doorway. Gods, he was terrifying. He scanned the scene with a soldier's precision before exchanging a few rapid, clipped words with the king. Then he turned and strode out again, his sword slung across his back like a promise of vengeance.

"You're safe now," Corvin said, voice low but fierce. "I'm sorry I wasn't here."

I shook my head weakly. "I'm fine. Really." I was lying, but I wanted to prove to him I could handle myself.

His eyes snapped to mine. "No, Liora. You're not."

Pain bloomed along my ribs. It was hot and sharp. I looked down to see the blood spreading on my shirt. Blood pooled beneath me, dark and slick against the sheets. My heartbeat stuttered. It wasn't just the pain that made my breath catch—it was the shock, the memory of Tyvlen's voice whispering, *kill the king*.

"We need to close it. Now, before you lose too much," Corvin said, voice taut but steady. "You don't heal as quickly as we do."

I tried to sit up, but the agony drove me back. Mimsy darted away, wings flashing, and returned moments later with a satchel clutched in her small hands, and another faerie trailing behind her. The newcomer's wings shimmered faintly, casting ripples of silver light across the blood-stained room. She met Corvin's eyes with a quiet nod before handing him a set of thin, gleaming tools.

Her voice, barely more than a whisper, broke the silence. "Hold her still. This will hurt."

Great. More pain. The needle pierced my flesh, and I cried out, tears streaming down my face. Corvin's hand found mine, warm and steady, squeezing gently. "You'll be fine," he whispered, though I could feel the worry in his voice.

The Faerie worked quickly, murmuring softly as she cleaned the wound, her tiny hands moving with precision. "Should take a few days, but it will heal quickly," she said, glancing up at Corvin with a nod of reassurance.

I closed my eyes, biting back a sob, letting Corvin's presence ground me. The room smelled faintly of herbs and blood, and I could hear the distant sounds of guards moving outside, still searching for the intruder. My chest ached, not just from pain, but from fear, and the realization of how close I had come to dying. Dying at the hands of Tyvlen, Maulgrove's little pet.

Corvin nodded to the faerie, who gathered her bag and disappeared as quickly as she had arrived. He stayed by my side, his hand still holding mine, brushing damp hair from my forehead. For the first time, the adrenaline faded, leaving me exhausted but grateful.

"I... I thought I lost you," he murmured, his voice barely above a whisper.

"You didn't," I said, my voice shaking. "I can handle myself."

He gave a faint, relieved smile, and I let myself rest, trusting him to keep me safe in a world that had suddenly grown far more dangerous than I'd imagined. I wanted to tell him it was Tyvlen who tried to kill me, but I was nervous he would be killed. I was afraid we would *all* be killed. Tyvlen's words repeated in my mind: *You will die, girl—by my hand, or another's. Fate is already sharpening the knife.* Were we in danger, or was this some sick game of his to get me to leave the king's side? Did Maulgrove and his clan truly want the throne? The questions gnawed at me, heavier than my wound. If they did, then Tyvlen's attack hadn't been random...it had been a warning. A message carved in flesh and blood.

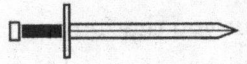

I awoke, sunlight glittering through the window. Corvin sat in the corner, a book clutched in his hands. I shot upright immediately, forgetting for a moment that I had been stabbed only hours ago.

"Ah, you're awake," he said, placing the book on the table with a soft thud, a small smile tugging at his lips. "Be careful, you're not fully healed yet."

I let out a shaky sigh. "That book... I found it in the—"

"In the library," he interrupted. "Under the floorboards."

I blinked, surprised he knew. "Yes, but... how did you know?"

He chuckled softly. "Because I saw it when I brought Mimsy to you. You may be sneaky, Liora, but I pay attention." His smile deepened. "Who do you think put it in the library?"

"You? You put it in the floor?"

"Well of course I did. I didn't think anyone would ever find it. Though, I suppose it isn't the best hiding spot for someone who enjoys snooping."

I cleared my throat. "Oh... right."

"I'm guessing you've taken a look inside?"

I nodded.

"Ah, so you have."

"Why didn't you get rid of it?" I asked, a tremor of unease in my voice. "It contains so many secrets and information that could be used against you."

Corvin's smile faltered slightly, replaced by a shadow of something heavier. "I thought I might keep it just in case I ever needed it." He paused, almost as if weighing whether to continue. "For what, I don't know. But some things are safer kept close, even if their purpose isn't immediately clear."

I glanced at the book on the table, its worn cover almost glowing in the sunlight. "It's strange. I read it, and it feels...personal. Almost like it knows things about you that no one else should. The girl who wrote it...she knew about the secrets of Nyriathee. She knew how to keep herself safe."

He nodded slowly. "It does. That book even holds my true name."

His voice was quiet, almost reverent. "Not the name the faeries of Nyriathee call me. My true name. It's dangerous knowledge. If it falls into the wrong hands..." He shook his head and ran a hand through his hair. "That's why I left it hidden. I didn't know who might find it, or when it might be needed."

I swallowed, the weight of his words pressing down on me. "So... you trust me to have it."

"I believe I do." He said simply, his eyes locking onto mine. "Something tells me I can trust you...that I should trust you. But that doesn't mean I don't want to make sure you're all right first." He stepped closer, glancing at the faint bruising around my side.

"I'm fine," I insisted, pressing a hand to the wound. "Really. It's nothing you need to fuss over."

He frowned, reaching out anyway. "You've been stabbed, Liora. I should—"

"No," I cut him off, more firmly this time. "I'll be okay. Don't worry about me. Not right now."

Corvin studied me for a long moment, his hand still hovering in the air as if debating whether to obey me or his instincts. Finally, he let it drop, but his gaze lingered on me with an intensity that made my skin prickle. "Very well," he said quietly. "But don't think I won't check later."

I smiled, "Thanks."

"Veyrix has not found the faerie who did this. But I intend to. No matter what it takes, I will put an end to their life."

I swallowed hard. I wanted to confess it was Tyvlen. I wanted to tell him that he was working with Maulgrove and Esmara, but I couldn't risk putting Corvin in danger. I wanted to kill Tyvlen myself. I wanted his blood on my hands. "Be careful, please."

Corvin's eyes shimmered. "You've been asking for a sword of your own for months... I guess I should have one made for you. As you said before, this blade won't do much."

I laughed. "Took a faerie almost taking my life for you to finally see that I do need a sword, huh?"

Corvin chuckled. "Be careful, little human. I might change my mind. Now rest and I will be back for you."

I lay back, watching him disappear through the doorway, the faintest trace of magic trailing behind him like smoke. My chest fluttered. It was half from fear, half from something I didn't dare name.

Just before my eyes closed, his voice drifted back, soft but certain. "Try not to dream of me, Liora. I'd hate to have to rescue you twice."

CHAPTER 16
THE WEIGHT
OF A CROWN

"It's someone who is in the castle. Someone who knows their way around," Mimsy said, breathing heavily; the tremor in her voice made it obvious she was frightened for her own safety.

"They don't have a name?" I asked, pretending ignorance.

"Not yet... but I think it's Tyvlen. Working for Maulgrove." Her words were barely a whisper.

I kept my face still. "They're looking for the faerie who did this."

Mimsy nodded. "They will be thorough."

"I heard Corvin say the same before he left. Said he would find them and kill them. He sent Veyrix."

I felt a sting of guilt for not telling Mimsy I already knew who it was, but fear clenched my tongue. Tyvlen had been around her a long time, but that asshole deserves what's coming to him.

Mimsy shivered. "What if they come back?"

"I don't think they'll try. I'm not the only one who is bleeding."

A knock sounded at the door. My heart tucked into my throat. The door opened and Tyvlen stepped in, a tray balanced in his hands. What the hell? The sight of him made my body shudder; he smiled with the kind of friendliness that never reached his eyes. "Food is here," he said, setting the tray on the table.

He offered a soft, polite smile to both of us.

Mimsy said nothing. Neither did I.

"Was he walking strangely?" Mimsy asked, brow furrowed.

"I didn't notice." I lied, forcing myself to stand, ignoring the pain in my side. "Let's eat. I need to heal so I'm ready for whatever happens next."

We ate—Mimsy perched on the table, me at the chair—sharing a meal that tasted like the one I had with Corvin in his chambers: sweet fruit, dripping with juice, and bread so tender it practically melted in my mouth. I ate until my stomach ached, until it begged for mercy, and still I could not stop. Inside me, something dark and bright at once unfurled. I would kill Tyvlen. His death would be mine alone.

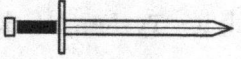

CORVIN HAD CALLED me to his chambers late that night. He was preparing for a celebration in the court and had offered me an invitation. Nervous but feeling much better, I agreed to go. My wound had almost completely healed, only small patches of skin still knitting themselves together.

Corvin waited outside my door as I got ready. Mimsy, as always, had fun picking out my outfit.

When I opened the door, Corvin bowed. "Beautiful."

Heat rushed to my cheeks. "You look lovely yourself, but I look better." I think he enjoyed my sarcasm, the way I always kept him on his toes.

"That you do, indeed," he said, extending his hand. I took it, and we stepped out together.

The court was more lively than the last time I had been there. Instead of going straight to his throne, Corvin got me a drink and walked around to greet some of the faeries who had arrived. He seemed different lately, as if someone else had taken his place. The angry, dangerous king I had first encountered was gone. It was as if he had grown softer, more understanding. More protective.

He glanced back at me several times, making sure I was safe. I smiled in return. He looked happier, as if the dark cloud that had once hung over him had begun to lift. It seemed like he was finally enjoying the sunlight instead of the stars.

But then, in the blink of an eye, he was gone. One moment he was at my side, chatting with a group of faeries, and the next he vanished. The crowd of glittering faces and laughter blurred around me as I stood alone where he had left me, gripping my glass tightly.

I swallowed, unsure whether he had disappeared on purpose, or if it had been my mistake somehow. My heart thumped painfully in my chest, the warmth of the earlier moments fading into a gnawing uncertainty. The court continued its celebration, oblivious, while I remained frozen, the echo of his presence lingering like a shadow that refused to vanish.

"You know," a familiar voice drawled from the shadows, smooth and dangerous, "there are whispers that the court has become *unbalanced* since you arrived."

I turned sharply, my heart lurching. Tyvlen stood near the fountain, a slender glass of dark liquid in his hand, his presence somehow both casual and menacing. The water in the fountain rippled at his feet, catching the torchlight and throwing fractured reflections across his face. Shit.

"Oh...hi," I said, forcing a smile, though unease clawed at my chest. My eyes darted through the crowd, searching for Corvin.

"You should not be here." His tone was cold, final, as if the very air around us could crack under his disapproval.

I swallowed, my throat dry. "Excuse me?"

"You heard me." His eyes, sharp and unnervingly bright, fixed on me. "Humans and faeries are not meant to be together. Not meant to stand side by side and rule. It would be a disgrace... for all of Nyriathee. There are others here who agree with me. They are armed. They are ready to take your life and the king's."

Shock rooted me to the spot, my pulse thundering in my ears. My mind scrambled for words, but none came.

"Liora!" Corvin's voice rang out over the crowd urgent.

Tyvlen's lips curved into a cruel grin, "Be careful, little human," he purred, his voice low. "The hunt has begun, and you smell like prey."

Before I could react, he turned, blending seamlessly into the crowd as though he had never been there at all.

Corvin finally reached me, concern softening his usual court composure. "There you are," he said, his voice gentle, though his gaze immediately registered my tension. "What's wrong?"

"It's nothing," I muttered, brushing away the tremor in my voice. "Can we... go somewhere else?"

He inclined his head. "I was just about to go to the front of the court to make a speech. Come with me."

"I don't think we should."

Corvin's face shifted, "Liora...tell me what has happened."

"I think we're...we're going to be attacked."

"Why do you think that?" He asked, shifting his eyes around the court.

My stomach twisted with unease as I scanned for any sign of Tyvlen. But the crowd seemed innocuous, unaware, or unwilling to warn me.

"I know you said you are your own protection, but I think we may need more than that."

Corvin nodded, "I only said that to you when we first met

because I wanted you to feel safe with me. A king does protect himself, but under certain circumstances, I can ask for more."

I nodded, swallowing hard, "You need too. Now."

He called upon Veryix who stood by his side almost instantly. "Liora here claims there is going to be an attack."

If Veyrix felt any concern at all, he was good at hiding it.

"Now, let us pretend all is well. We do not want to stir any worry in my court."

At the throne, Corvin gestured for me to sit to the side, away from the direct line of the court's watchful eyes. He straightened, clearing his throat, and began speaking, his voice echoing through the hall with calm authority. I watched him, but my mind remained elsewhere, replaying Tyvlen's words like a blade cutting through my thoughts.

The words of the speech floated past me, about unity and the prosperity of Nyriathee, but I could barely focus. My eyes strained for any hint of movement, any shadow that might signal Tyvlen's return. My fingers clenched in my lap, knuckles white, and I forced myself to breathe. Every step, every word, every glance felt like a test of courage I wasn't sure I had. I peered around the court as the faeries gazed up at their king.

"Now let us celebrate!" Corvin shouted, "Celebrate the stars!"

Just as he finished, my eyes snagged on a hulking silhouette pushing through the crowd. Maulgrove. A single, deliberate shout split the court; it sounded engineered to scatter calm like glass. Tyvlen's grin flashed in my memory—this was his game: to seed panic and watch the world unravel. The hunt had begun in earnest. Fear pooled in my chest until it spilled out of me in a raw, high cry, hopeful and desperate all at once. "They're going to kill the king!" My eyes darted to Corvin, who was scanning the crowd. Chaos erupted—faeries crying, shouting, panicking.

An arrow shot from the ceiling, missing me by inches. I screamed, throwing myself to the side. Corvin charged toward me, sword drawn, his expression dark with anger.

Small faerie creatures I had never seen before scattered across the marble floor, their wings shimmering. Food and drink flew into the air as goblets toppled, platters crashed, and faeries darted in every direction, shouting and screaming. Arrows whizzed past my head, still unlucky.

Corvin swung his blade with precision, cutting down several of the arrows before they could cause any real damage. I staggered to my feet, steadying myself, and revealed my blade with trembling fingers. From the throne, the court looked entirely different—larger, more spacious, with shadows pooling in every corner. Perfect places for someone to hide.

My gaze lifted to the dark beams arching across the ceiling. I squinted, forcing myself to focus, and then I saw her. Esmara. She stood balanced with inhuman grace, a longbow clutched in her hands, a wicked grin stretching across her face. When our eyes met, she smiled. Her teeth were sharper than knives. She winked, then pulled back her arrow and shot it with lethal intent.

"Look out!" I screamed, shoving Corvin to the side.

The arrow struck through the empty throne with a sharp *crack*.

"Esmara!" I shrieked, tracking her as she darted across the ceiling beams, moving with the agility of a spider.

Corvin's eyes narrowed. His hand darted beneath his cloak and withdrew a dagger, gleaming under the torchlight. With a swift motion, he hurled it. The blade struck true, burying itself in the center of her back. Esmara screamed, her body twisting as she plummeted to the court floor. Blood spread in a dark pool beneath her, staining the polished stone. The crowd surged away from her body, desperate to escape the chaos.

Maulgrove knelt at her side, his massive frame hunched, his face twisted with rage and something darker. His hand lingered over her wound, trembling with fury as he looked up at us and pulled the dagger from her flesh.

"You will pay for this," he hissed, his voice low, venomous, "Both of you."

Before either of us could move, Maulgrove surged forward like a beast unleashed. He slammed into Corvin with bone-crushing force, sending him crashing against the base of his throne. Corvin's sword clattered across the floor, too far for him to reach.

Maulgrove raised a jagged blade, the black steel humming with dark energy, and brought it down toward my chest.

"No!" I heard Corvin scream.

He didn't think—he acted. With a wild cry, he leapt onto Maulgrove's back. Maulgrove roared, thrashing, but Corvin clung to him, his arm wrapping tight around his throat. Maulgrove's heavy body tossed Corvin into the air and he landed with a thud.

"Fools!" Maulgrove roared, spit flying from his mouth, "All of you! You think the light of the stars will save you? When I return, I'll take back what should be mine!" He pointed his sword in Corvin's direction, "Just as I took your dragon, I will take your throne."

The court fell into silence, broken only by the labored breaths of the few who remained. Mimsy stood amongst the crowd, her eyes wide with tears as she watched what had unfolded.

I lay against the cold, stone floor, my eyes studying Corvin. Blood trickled down his arm. He had been struck by Maulgrove's blade, the wound deep, and crimson poured freely down his side. His chest rose and fell, ragged with exhaustion, yet his gaze burned, unyielding.

"I will not falter," Corvin growled, voice carrying like thunder through the cavernous hall. "To save Nyriathee, to save those I love —I will bleed, I will burn, I will break every chain this darkness casts. But I will not fail. Try and kill me if you must, but you will be the one greeted by death."

Maulgrove reached the far end of the court, where his dragon, Tharion, awaited. The beast watched the chaos unfold with eerie calm, as though it, too, delighted in the ruin its master had sown.

I glanced back at Corvin and he collapsed, his blade stabbing into the stone floor with such force the chamber seemed to tremble. The clang echoed, sharp and final, as if the Court of Starlight itself bore witness to its king's fall. Blood pooled beneath him, dark against the pale stone, yet his grip on the hilt never loosened. Even broken, even bleeding from Maulgrove's cruel strike, Corvin's will refused to yield.

He lifted his head, eyes locking with mine, starlight dimming but unextinguished. "If this is the end...then let it be said I fought for Nyriathee. And for you, Liora."

CHAPTER 17
ESCAPE

"You will be safe far away from here." Mimsy said, dragging a small bag across the chamber floor with her teeth.

"I'm not leaving." I insisted.

Mimsy gave me a worried look, her ears flattening as though she could already sense the danger clawing at the walls. "You must, Liora! You must!"

"I cannot leave him. I cannot leave any of you."

"The king will be fine," Mimsy pressed, her small voice trembling with urgency. "He is in good hands. He will be protected. You will not be."

Her eyes darted toward the door, pupils dilating. "Please—hurry, before—"

The chamber doors slammed open with a thunderous crack, splinters flying. Shadows spilled into the room like ink, and Tyvlen's tall figure emerged, his armor glinting coldly in the torchlight.

Mimsy let out a cry and darted in front of me, her tiny body bristling, tail puffed out like a plume of smoke. "Run, Liora!" she shrieked. Tyvlen reached forward and smacked Mimsy.

I barely took a step before Tyvlen's hand closed around my arm, strong and merciless. I struggled, clawing at his grip, but he only laughed, low and cruel, lifting me off the ground as though I weighed nothing.

"Mimsy, no—!" I screamed as I watched her small, fragile figure lunge at him, sinking her teeth into his hand. He flung her aside with a vicious sweep of his arm, sending her skidding across the stone floor once again.

"You thought you could hide her from me?" Tyvlen's voice echoed through the chamber, dark and triumphant. His eyes burned with a twisted hunger as he dragged me toward the gaping doorway.

"Liora!" Mimsy cried, scrambling weakly to her feet. "Hold on—!"

But Tyvlen's shadow swallowed us both as he vanished into the night, my cries silenced beneath his hand, leaving Mimsy alone in the broken chamber.

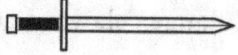

All I remembered was the sting of my body scraping against the damp forest floor of Nyriathee. The earth was soft with recent rain, clinging to my skin, and the air was heavy with the cloying sweetness of honey. My rowan berries scattered into the shadows, torn from my neck, yet the mirror shard pressed cold and certain against my chest, hidden in my pocket.

Then I heard her. It was my sister's voice, raw and sharp as it cut through the haze. *Liora!* Her cry carried not in fear but in laughter. I saw her, radiant, strawberry hair streaming as if the wind itself had chosen her as its muse. Flowers burst to life at her feet, unfolding in colors too bright for this darkness. Her smile was both salvation and torment, because it was impossible, because it was her.

My mind reeled, latching not to pain, but to sorrow. To him. Corvin—his breath warm against my neck, his hands tracing the curve of my spine, the rhythm of our bodies as if they had always known each other. I remembered the weight of him, the heat, the way the world had seemed to dissolve until only our gasps remained. The ache of wanting him. The ache of loving him. The thoughts came in fragments, a fevered montage, too sharp, too alive for the nightmare I was trapped in.

"Sit up!" Tyvlen commanded, his voice sharp. He shoved me against the rough bark of a tree. "I'll get the dragon if I have too."

I staggered, my body begging for sleep.

"I said, sit up!" he cried again, this time seizing the cloth of my shirt, the fabric stretching as though afraid of his touch.

"Get off of me." I managed to breathe, pushing my hand against his.

"The king will come searching, little human. He will crawl upon his knees like a starved child, mewling for forgiveness that will not come."

I smirked through my exhaustion. "He'll kill you."

Tyvlen's laughter rang out, crystalline and cruel, carrying a music that made my skin crawl. "Kill me? Oh, I would pay in silver and sorrow to watch him try."

"He did just kill Esmara—"

"Do not speak her name!" Tyvlen hissed, and the air itself seemed to recoil, branches above us creaking. "Her name is not yours to touch with your human tongue. I warned you. I warned you of the ruin your kind drags behind them like chains. Nyriathee wilts beneath your shadow."

His hand pressed harder into my shoulder, his fingers cold as river stone. His eyes gleamed, pupils thin and glinting like mirror shards.

"And yet," I whispered, forcing the words past the weight of his presence, "you remain. Isn't that strange?"

"Strange?" His lips parted in a smile both beautiful and terrible. "No, not strange. I linger because your fate is a thread wound through mine. The king's blood burns with your stain now. Every breath you take unravels another stitch of this realm's tapestry."

"I never asked for this," I spat, my defiance small but sharp.

Tyvlen tilted his head, voice dipping into something almost mournful. "No soul asks for their doom. Doom comes unbidden, as sure as twilight. It knocks at your ribs until you let it in. And you—" he leaned closer, his breath cool as midnight—"you opened the door wide."

The earth shuddered beneath us, a slow groan, as if roots deep below strained to hold their ground. Tyvlen's smile faltered, though only for the briefest flicker of a moment.

"If doom has chosen me," I whispered, "then perhaps it has chosen you too."

Tyvlen tilted his head, "Chosen me? Human girl, I am the teeth of doom, not its prey. You misunderstand. I do not fall beneath its shadow. I *cast* it."

I met his dark eyes, my throat raw but my words sharp, tears streaming down my face. "You think yourself untouchable. But the truth is this...the king never loved Evelyn. He only used her. And she —" I let the venom drip, slow and deliberate, "she never loved you, Tyvlen. Because she saw you for what you are. A disgusting monster." I knew there was a reason he hated the king. I had thought myself into a spiral trying to put the pieces together. Evelyn loved the king. The king didn't love her. Tyvlen, the poor servant to the king, fell in love with a human girl who wanted nothing to do with him. Greedy bastard.

His smile shattered. Not into laughter, but into something far more dangerous. His voice dropped low. "Monster, am I? Ah, little thorn-tongue, you wield cruelty like a blade, but you do not know where you cut." His hand slid from my shoulder to my throat, hovering like a promise. "Do you think love is a thing your kind alone can claim? Evelyn drank from my cup of devotion, even as she spat it back upon me. She knew me. She *feared* me. And fear—ah, fear is closer to love than your human heart dares to admit."

His eyes gleamed, wet as though some ancient sorrow flickered behind the fury. But his grin returned, cruel and sharp. "Call me monster if you wish. But monsters, like the dragons and I, are what shape kingdoms. Not lovers."

His hand lashed forward, gripping my collar, dragging me so close I could see the black veins spidering in his golden eyes. "Tell me," he hissed, "how do you *know* of her?"

My lips trembled, but I forced them into a defiant curve. "Scriptwight told me."

The effect was immediate. His fingers clenched, then loosened, as if my very words had burned him. He staggered back half a step, his face flickering with shock. His voice cracked with a mixture of rage and disbelief.

"Scriptwight?" he repeated, as though tasting the name was poison. "That wretch dares to whisper her truths into your ears?"

But even as he raged, his façade cracked further. His chest heaved, his jaw tight. His eyes, for the briefest moment, glistened with something rawer than anger. I was making progress. The words were torture.

"Evelyn..." he whispered, almost too soft to hear, as if the name itself could break him. Then his fury surged again, covering the fracture. "You know nothing of her. Nothing of what bound us. And if you speak her name again, human, I will tear the voice from your throat."

I swallowed, rubbing my head against the rough tree behind me.

"Enough!" Maulgrove's voice was deep, and powerful, making us both jump.

He stepped from the shadows, dragging his leg as if he had been injured in the court. "I have a few things to say before we do away with her."

Tyvlen stepped back as if he obeyed every word, "Be quick. I want to see her suffer!"

I swallowed, the edges of my vision shimmering. Rage was a hot thing in my chest, but it steadied into a ledge I could climb on. "There's only one throne," I said, my voice cutting through the night even as my hands trembled. "And it isn't built for murder and lies."

Maulgrove laughed, "Thrones belong to the strong," he said, "To those who take them. To those who deserve them."

"Then Tyvlen can keep polishing the steps," I sneered. "He'll always be the king's footman. Fetching and fawning. He'll never be a king himself."

Tyvlen's expression flickered, hurt, then fury, before he masked it with a sneer. Maulgrove's smile widened, like a crack spreading on an icy pond, "Such spirit," he purred. "It makes this all the more entertaining. No wonder the king enjoys your company."

He turned slowly, the faintest smirk twisting his mouth, "Ah," Maulgrove murmured, "I almost forgot my companion."

From behind the trees, the ground trembled with a low, rumbling quake that made the air itself shudder. Branches snapped like bones, and a shadow uncoiled between the trunks. Tharion emerged, enormous and terrible, his scales slick and eyes burning with molten gold. The forest seemed to bow away from him; even the night went quiet.

Maulgrove lifted a hand and Tharion's massive head dipped in acknowledgement, a sound like thunder rolling from deep in his chest.

"Remember tonight, girl," Maulgrove hissed. "When the court falls and the world burns, you and the king will have each other in death."

He climbed onto the dragon's back with a slow, eerie grace. As Tharion spread its wings, the rush of wind scattered leaves in a storm of silver moonlight. The world went still, the dragon's eyes burning a hole through me. Desperation, maybe. A look of a longing to escape.

Then they rose, vanishing through the trees and into the dark sky. The silence that followed was a living thing, brittle, stunned, and terribly fragile. I had yet to see someone ride a dragon. It was magnificent as much as it was terrifying. Through Maulgrove's conversation, I almost forgot about Tyvlen who was still watching me closely.

He smiled into my direction, leaning down close to my face, "I met your sister, you know."

The words struck me, and I forgot about the dragon, "What did you say?"

A wicked smile formed on Tyvlen's face. "Ah, yes, your precious little sister. Elsie? That is her name. Isn't it?"

"What did you do to her?" I screamed, tears rolling down my cheeks as I lunged forward. I wanted to wrap my hands around his throat and squeeze until he went limp.

"I didn't do anything." He sneered. "Esmara is the one who said she was weak."

I squirmed, the binding around my wrists tight against my back. "No, please! Don't hurt her."

Tyvlen smiled. "Oh human girl, Esmara only warned her of your fate. Apparently she shattered like a million stars."

His words slithered into me like poison, hollowing out my chest. My pulse hammered, every breath shallow and ragged. "You're lying," I whispered, though my voice cracked with fear.

"Am I?" His eyes glinted in the moonlight like a predator. "She begged for you. Cried your name. Do you want to hear her last word?"

"No!" The scream tore from my throat, desperate, breaking.

Tyvlen leaned closer, his breath warm and rotten against my ear. "Help."

My heart lurched, a jagged shard of hope stabbing through the despair. If Elsie had run, maybe—just maybe—she was still out there somewhere.

"Esmara didn't forgive weakness," Tyvlen continued, standing tall again, his smile a blade of malice. "And neither do I."

"Corvin will kill you!" I snapped, lunging toward Tyvlen's face.

"Who?" He whispered, slithering back like a snake.

I stuttered, nervous about what I had just said, "Uh...the king. He will...kill you."

"Corvin?" He smiled, "So you know his true name?"

I shook my head, playing stupid.

Tyvlen grabbed me by the shirt and lifted me into the air, "Tell me his true name!"

"I—I don't know!" I shouted, turning my face away from his.

"Put her down. Now."

A small squeak came from a hollow in the tree ahead. The shadows of the night made it hard to see, but the voice was unmistakable.

Mimsy.

She stepped into the faint glow, her tiny frame squared with defiance."Tyvlen. Put. Her. Down."

Tyvlen laughed, low and cruel. "And what will you do about it, you pathetic little rat?"

Mimsy's face twisted with fury. "Veyrix!"

From the darkness, a monstrous figure emerged. It was Veyrix, towering higher than even the oldest trees. Tyvlen faltered, his grip on my shirt loosening. Mimsy must have gone to Corvin, must have told him of my abduction. They had come for me. I was a human who didn't belong, yet they were here to save my life.

Before Tyvlen shoved me aside to run, he leaned close, his breath icy against my ear. For the first time, he spoke my name. "Death will come quickly, Liora. Your precious king will grieve your loss, and Maulgrove and I will take his crown."

Veyrix's massive hand closed around Tyvlen's throat, lifting him as if he weighed nothing. His voice, deeper than I imagined, rumbled through the night. "Tyvlen, I bring a message from the king."

Even strangled, Tyvlen smirked.

"The king says you are to leave and never return. The Court of Starlight no longer claims you. You are exiled."

Veyrix released him, and Tyvlen crumpled, gasping for air.

Clutching his bruised neck, he still found words. "Tell your foolish king that I killed Evelyn. Tell Corvin...yes, that was his name, wasn't it?" His eyes cut toward me, and Mimsy gasped.

"That is correct," Veyrix rumbled.

So Veyrix has known the king's first name all along. I wonder if he knows his *true name*.

Tyvlen's laugh was jagged, inhuman. "Stupid human girl. You've doomed Nyriathee. You've doomed the Court of Starlight. You've doomed them all!"

I said nothing, but Mimsy pressed herself against my leg.

"The king doesn't want you," he sneered. "You're nothing more than the next girl to fall under his enchantment."

Rage boiled in my chest, spilling out before I could stop it. "You —" I lunged, reaching for his throat, but Veyrix caught the back of my shirt and held me suspended. "You vile, wretched monster! I'll see your blood spilt, and I'll do it myself!"

Veyrix's eyes flicked to me, the faintest smile curving his lips.

Still holding me aloft, he turned back to Tyvlen. "The king says if you shed even a single drop of her blood, he will find you in exile and end your pathetic life."

Tyvlen's skin had already darkened to a sickly purple where Veyrix's grip had crushed him. He said nothing more, but his wicked smile lingered as he slunk into the woods.

Veyrix picked up Mimsy gently, then swung me up in his other arm, carrying us both back into the night.

For a fleeting moment, I thought I saw her...my sister...standing among the trees, framed by glowing pink and violet flowers. But I knew it was only my imagination, playing cruel tricks on me.

CHAPTER 18

THE DUEL OF STARLIGHT

When I returned to the castle, King Corvin stood near the entrance, his sword planted into the ground like a crutch. The stiffness in his stance told me his side was still aching from the recent attack in the court. Now I understood why he didn't come looking for me himself.

"Veyrix, you may rest," he said, nodding with approval.

Veyrix lowered Mimsy first, then me. Corvin smiled warmly at Mimsy, "I want to thank you, and apologize for how I treated you."

Mimsy didn't say anything, but she bowed before scurrying off into the castle, leaving only Corvin and I at the entrance.

"Liora..." His golden eyes shimmered. "You are safe."

I nodded, smoothing the wrinkles from my shirt. "I am."

"May we speak in my chambers, away from the ears of others?"

I swallowed the nervous tension rising in my throat and smiled faintly. "Of course."

He extended his hand, as he had the first night we met. This time, I trusted him enough to take it without hesitation.

We walked through the long halls, faeries' curious eyes following us as we passed certain rooms. In the library, I glimpsed Scriptwight flipping through a book. He glanced up, nodded once, and I knew he was acknowledging me.

"Come in, please," Corvin said, opening the door to his chambers.

I obeyed. "How's your—?"

Before I could finish, he interrupted. "Do not worry about me. Tell me what happened. I want to hear it from you."

"Well..." I began, settling onto the edge of his large bed.

A knock at the door cut me short.

"Yes?" Corvin called, his brow furrowing.

"Who is that?" I whispered, uneasy that he wasn't expecting anyone.

"I'm not entirely sure..." he murmured, tiptoeing to the door.

"King, sir," came Scriptwight's voice, "I found this small, human child sneaking through the castle."

My heart slammed in my chest as Corvin pulled the door open. Over his broad shoulder, I saw my sister, Elsie, clutched tightly in Scriptwight's grip.

Is this real? "Elsie!" I cried, bursting past Corvin, nearly knocking him aside.

Scriptwight recoiled in surprise as Elsie and I collided, our arms wrapping tightly around each other.

"What? How?" The words tumbled out of me, broken and desperate.

She loosened her grip but kept her hands on my shoulders. Her eyes were wide, her face pale. "I don't know how I got here. There was this creature. It had long, green hair, and glowing eyes. She said I had to come with her."

My breath caught. *Esmara.*

The name curled like poison in my mind. *Esmara.* She had taken Elsie. She had brought her here. And what Tyvlen had warned me of was true.

"Are you hurt?" I shrieked, scanning her from head to toe.

"No..." she whispered, shaking her head. "But she wasn't gentle."

I spun toward Corvin, my voice trembling with anger. "But you killed Esmara. I saw you. I saw the dagger strike her."

Corvin's jaw tightened as he nodded. "Yes. I did. But this must have been—"

"When?" I cut in sharply. "When did they do this to you?"

Elsie's brow furrowed in confusion. "I...I don't really know."

I exhaled shakily, pulling her close once more. "It must have been before the attack in the court the other night. I'm just so glad you're safe."

"Safe," Scriptwight muttered from the doorway, "is not a word to rely on here."

"I know," I admitted, my eyes locking desperately with him. "I need Mimsy. Please."

Scriptwight glanced at Corvin, silently reminding me that no one in Nyriathee, least of all a human, could command him.

The king inclined his head. "Fetch Mimsy. Tell her it is urgent."

Scriptwight bowed and slipped out, closing the door behind him.

Corvin strode to a nearby table and poured himself a drink, taking a slow sip. The movement drew Elsie's wary gaze, her eyes wide with shock and amusement. I knew the look because I felt it too when I first arrived.

"What is this place?" she breathed.

A wry smile tugged at my lips. "This is Nyriathee." I gestured toward Corvin. "And this is its king."

Corvin gave her a curt nod before raising his glass again.

Suddenly, Mimsy scurried through the small crack at the bottom of the door, her whiskers twitching. "What's happened?" she asked breathlessly.

Her eyes landed on Elsie, and she froze. "Liora, there are two of you?"

I laughed despite the heaviness in my chest. "No, Mimsy. This is my sister. Her name is Elsie."

Mimsy's shocked expression remained. She said nothing, only studied her intently.

"Hi, little creature," Elsie said softly, kneeling down to greet her. "You look like a chipmunk."

Mimsy froze, her dark eyes widening. Her voice trembled. "I am glamoured. How did you...how did you know?"

Elsie blinked. "I don't know."

Corvin's golden eyes flicked to me. "She has the Sight."

"What?" I asked, my heart lurching.

"The Sight," he repeated, his tone certain. "She sees Nyriathee for what it truly is. Not the veil, not the glamour. The truth. Just as you do, Liora."

Mimsy gasped, pressing her tiny paws against her mouth. "The Sight? In this child? But Liora—"

"How do we both have it?" I whispered, realization chilling me to the bone. "Where did it come from?"

Elsie's gaze darted around the chamber, her expression tightening. "This isn't really a castle at all. It's... it's ruined. The walls look like they're rotting, the air is damp. Everything is crumbling, Liora. Can't you see it?"

I could see it. All of it. The horror of it all, but most of the time, I turned it off. All I wanted to see was the sweeping stone arches, the golden torchlight flickering across carved walls, the gleam of Corvin's polished table. Beautiful. Enchanted. Untouched.

"Yes." I said faintly. "But I like to see it for what the king has made it to be."

Corvin stepped forward, his face grave. "The Sight is spoken of as a rare curse, or a blessing, depending on who tells the tale of it. Those who possess it can pierce glamour, unravel illusions, and step where humans were never meant to walk. They are the only ones who see the Fae for what we are." His gaze lingered on Elsie. "It is why we fear them. And why some of us would claim them." He cleared his throat, "It is passed down in the family, usually from the mother's side."

"No one is claiming my sister," I snapped. "She shouldn't even be here. She was brought against her will." Then I paused, realizing what he said. "Wait, does that mean my mother...?"

Corvin nodded. Mimsy gasped.

"Your mother has the Sight also. She has given it to you."

"Well..." Elsie spoke, "I hate to bring bad news."

My head whipped toward her. "What?"

"I went out searching for you," she admitted, her voice small but steady. "You haven't been home in ages. Mom and Dad called the police. There are posters, commercials, and searches. Everyone thinks you're the next missing girl from town."

I exhaled, the weight of her words pressing down like stone. "Right..."

Elsie shrugged lightly, trying to mask her worry. "But now that I've found you, we can go."

I glanced at Corvin. Something inside of me admitted that I didn't want to leave him behind.

"Elsie," I said carefully, "I can't just leave."

"What?" Mimsy piped up with a laugh. "Of course you can."

My stomach dropped. "No, I...I don't want to."

Corvin swallowed hard, his jaw tightening. "May I speak honestly?"

I turned toward him, nodding.

He stood up straight, "I want to keep you here. You are different, Liora. You are—"

"I am what?" I asked.

Elsie's voice interrupted the moment. "Why do you look..." She trailed off, squinting at Corvin.

"What?" I demanded, turning on her.

"Him," she said, pointing at Corvin. "He's the only thing in this place that doesn't look...like it wants to kill me. Other than the chipmunk of course."

"Mimsy." Mimsy squeaked, reminding my sister of her name.

My breath caught. "What are you talking about?"

"The others. The faeries I've seen here. They sort of look like something out of a horror movie. Twisted. Wrong. But him?" She tilted her head. "He looks... normal. Cute, even."

Despite myself, a smile tugged at my lips. "Cute?"

"Yeah," she said with a half-smile. "Handsome, even. Like one of those guys on TV. You know, Liora—the guy from *Gilmore*—"

"Yes, I know who you're talking about," I interrupted quickly, my face burning.

Corvin shifted uncomfortably as I turned back to him. "So if we both have the Sight, passed down from my mother...why don't you look like the others?"

"Because," Corvin said evenly, "I do not glamour myself. I am half human, half faerie."

Finally, he had admitted it. It was true. That's why he looked different from the others. They must hate him for it, being half human.

"I want you to see me as I truly am."

Mimsy let out a high-pitched giggle from the floor.

I narrowed my eyes. "So you really do look as I see you?"

"Try the mirror shard," he said quietly.

My hand trembled as I reached into my pocket, pulling out the shard. I hadn't used it. I didn't need to. I wiped the dirt from its surface and lifted it, angling it toward him. His reflection stared back at me—golden eyes, sharp jaw, pointed ears, and all.

The same as what I saw with my own eyes, even if I turned the Sight off. He was *handsome. So incredibly damn handsome.*

"So...how do we leave?" Elsie asked, interrupting the moment once more.

"We can go to another room. I think we should." Mimsy said through her nervous giggles.

"Please, don't go." Corvin said, "Liora, please."

"What is it you really want from me?"

He cleared his throat and stepped toward me, grabbing hold of both my hands. "You think I do not see it, Liora? The stars burn in your eyes, and every time you defy me, I feel myself pulled into their gravity... helpless, no matter how I fight it."

I didn't know what to say. I stood there frozen, staring back at him. We had been enemies, unsure of one another, and now in this moment, everything felt different. Changed.

"Don't you see, Liora? Every breath you take stirs something restless inside me. Every word you speak is a spell I cannot break. You haunt me in silence and in the way you defy me. I am undone by the thought of losing you before I have even held you. I swore to keep my heart bound in stone, but you—" his voice faltered, tightening with raw feeling, "you slipped through every crack, every fracture in my defenses, until you are the very marrow of me."

He squeezed my hands, his thumb brushing along my knuckles as if memorizing them. "You are the flame that sets the night ablaze, the thorn that makes me bleed, and yet I crave your touch still. You are ruin and salvation in the same breath, and I—" He leaned closer, his forehead nearly resting against mine. "I would rather be destroyed by loving you than live untouched by your fire."

Both Mimsy and Elsie's mouths hung open as if they were watching a movie. I knew they felt it, because I felt it too.

"I—uh..." I didn't know what to say.

"Liora, do not leave me."

The moment was broken by screams from down the hall. Scriptwight burst through the door, followed by Veyrix.

"They are here for blood!"

I grabbed my sister, "Under the bed, now!"

Both my sister and Mimsy did as I said and scurried under the bed, shielding themselves from the chaos.

Corvin pulled his sword from its sheath, "Who?"

Veyrix's voice boomed, shaking the very walls of the room, "Tyvlen and Maulgrove! They are here. In the court!"

The Court of Starlight. He was here to take the throne. Just as they said. Those evil assholes. I hope they were ready for a battle, because I'm not going down without one.

"Corvin!" I shouted, grabbing a small dagger from a shelf in the room. The king turned, his expression wild with concern, "They're here to kill us."

"I know." Corvin said, "But I will kill them both before they even get the chance."

We rushed through the halls, faeries running past us, screams of horror filling the empty spaces. When we stepped into the Court of Starlight, Tyvlen was in the middle of the stone floor, blood splattered across it. Bodies of at least 10 faeries lie still, dead.

"Here for the celebration, king?" He screamed, blood dripping from the blade in his hand, "You're late!"

I gasped, tears rolling down my cheeks as I studied the lifeless bodies on the floor around him. I thought they were all faeries at first, but one of them had been human.

"Tyvlen..." Corvin said, "You have been exiled. You are not welcome here."

He stepped closer, advancing toward us, "Exiled? The only way to exile me is to kill me."

Corvin spoke once more, warning him, "Leave, now. And no more blood will have to be shed."

Tyvlen didn't say anything, instead, he looked past us with an odd expression. "Elsie!" He hissed, "You made it."

I spun around and saw my sister standing at the doorway of the court, watching the terror unfold.

"No!" I screamed, "You need to run!"

But she didn't. She stood there, crying. I knew she was horrified by the scene in front of her. The blood. The bodies. The smell of rot. I glanced up as the stars themselves began to fade.

"I'll make you a deal, Liora." Tyvlen snarled, "You give me your sister, and I'll let you live with this sad excuse of a king."

Corvin spoke before I had the chance, "She is with me. As is Liora, as is Mimsy, as was Evelyn."

"Evelyn should have been mine!" Tyvlen roared, lifting his sword. "And now you parade another fragile little human in her place? How many will you ruin before they see you for the coward you truly are?"

Tyvlen swung, his blade whistling past Corvin by inches.

"Stand down, Tyvlen," Corvin warned, raising his sword. "This won't end well for you."

I sucked in a breath, holding the small dagger steady in my hand. I felt a spark of anger against Corvin for not getting me a sword, but the dagger would have to do.

"Wont end well for me?" Tyvlen laughed, a chilling sound. "I will cut your head off in front of everyone here! In front of all of Nyriathee! In front of the Court of Starlight! In front of your new pet!"

"I do not wish to hurt you," Corvin said, "but I will if I must."

"You are a disgrace to the court!" Tyvlen shouted, swinging again, "You aren't even a true faerie!"

"You'll eat your words!" I shouted, trying to sound tough.

Tyvlen ignored me as if I weren't even there. His sole focus was to kill the king.

Before anyone could react, Tyvlen lifted his blade, swinging it toward Corvin. I raised my tiny blade and threw it, watching it sail toward Tyvlen's body. He dodged it, and raised his sword once more, slicing across Corvin's arm. Corvin let out a shriek of unexpected pain and dropped his sword, clutching the wound as blood blossomed between his fingers. The rest of the crowd in the court erupted with screams, laughter, and crying—fear, shock, and excitement blending into a deafening roar.

Corvin steadied himself and lifted his sword again, slashing at Tyvlen and cutting through the right side of his shirt. Through the crowd, I caught sight of Mimsy, tears streaming down her face. I lost sight of her for a moment, then she appeared between the legs of a tall faerie with dark green skin.

"Liora!" she screamed, as if calling me to her. But I couldn't leave Corvin. Not now. I had to save them all.

Tyvlen must have heard Mimsy's cry because he turned sharply, a cruel smile twisting across his face. "Goodbye, little rat."

Mimsy spun to flee, but she didn't make it two steps before she crumpled. Her small body hit the stone floor with a hollow sound, deep red spreading beneath her like a blooming flower.

"No!" The scream tore from my throat before I could stop it, raw and shaking, as if her pain had ripped straight through me. The world seemed to spin—her laughter, her warmth, her friendship, gone in an instant, leaving only silence and the echo of her fall.

I grabbed at my chest, my breath heaving. I had lost my friend. The only true friend I had made in Nyriathee.

Tyvlen hissed, turning back to the king, "You are no king. You will die a coward. A failure."

Corvin must have seen what had happened to Mimsy, because he faltered and Tyvlen took advantage of the moment, striking and slicing across Corvin's leg. Corvin screamed, his sword clanging to the ground. Blood spattering across the throne, the jewels shimmering in deep red. His crown tilted dangerously, bending one ear painfully.

I had to act. But my sister beat me to it. Tyvlen stood still, staring down at the blade shoved through his chest. He was coughing up blood, lots of it. He reached down to pull the blade out, but instead, he fell to the ground, the blade in my sister's hand. Badass.

Suddenly, the ground began to shake. "Elsie!" I screamed, "You must run! Hide! I will find you!"

She dropped the blade, scurrying to the corner of the room.

Maulgrove entered, his monstrous frame filling the empty space. Tharion gripped the metallic star on top of the castle, looking down on the scene.

"Ah... the human girl thinks herself brave enough to kill us both? Foolish child."

"I'm not afraid of you, Maulgrove." I said, stepping forward, my voice steady despite my pounding heart. "You will kill no one today. It will be your blood that is shed in this court."

He sneered, circling me like a predator. "You? You are nothing. You are a toy. A puppet for the king. You cannot stop me."

"I am nothing to fear," I said, gripping the dagger in my hands, feeling the pulse of everything the king had taught me—the stance, the balance, the patience. "But I *can* end your life."

Maulgrove lunged, his blade slicing through the air. I dodged instinctively, rolling to the side, feeling the cold stone bite my palms. Corvin groaned behind me, gripping his wounded leg, but I didn't stop.

I saw Corvin's sword lying on his throne. My eyes locked on it. *The lessons, the practice... now.* I had never used it before. He had never even let me feel its weight in my human hands. I dove for it, grabbing the hilt and rising it as Maulgrove came at me again. It was heavier than I had expected, and I almost couldn't bear the weight of it. His eyes widened. It was clear he hadn't expected me to take the weapon.

"You think that will save you?" he hissed.

"Not save me," I said, meeting his gaze. "Finish what you started... on *your terms*. The debt must be balanced."

He swung with a roar, and I blocked, parrying his strikes with every motion Corvin had drilled into me. Step, pivot, counter. I felt the rhythm of the fight, the surge of focus. Maulgrove sneered and pressed harder, but I was ready.

Finally, he overextended. I pivoted, drove my strength into the blade, and struck at the exposed side beneath his ribs. The sword sank in deep. He gasped, eyes wide, disbelief flooding his features.

"Gotchya!" I said, mockingly in my human tone.

He collapsed, the sword clattering from his grasp. The court fell silent, the chaos freezing in suspended shock. I stood over him, chest heaving, blood on my hands and on Corvin's blade.

"You underestimated me," I said quietly, my voice steady despite the adrenaline. "Now you will die like the coward you are."

Maulgrove's body crumpled, the life leaving him in slow, cruel waves, "A half-faerie king, and a human, what a disgrace."

The court was frozen in stunned silence, broken only by muffled sobs and the metallic scent of blood heavy in the air. My hands trembled as I let Corvin's sword fall, my chest heaving from the fight. What struck me most was how Maulgrove's dragon didn't lash out at his master's defeat. Instead, it lifted its head and released a roar that sent flames skittering across the night sky. Then it turned to me, its gaze lingering, as if in silent gratitude.

"You are free." I said, nodding my head.

Tharion let out a great sigh before soaring upward and vanishing into the darkness of the night.

I turned to face Corvin. He was on his knees, blood soaking through his clothes. The wound on his leg and the slash across his arm left him pale, barely holding himself upright. Panic clawed at my chest. I ran to him, my legs moving as if on fire. He never taught me how to heal the Fae. Gods, why didn't he teach me anything other than how to wield a blade? I glanced over to the spot where Mimsy's lifeless body lay, the ache in my chest a reminder of a piece of me I had already lost.

"Corvin! Hold on!" I cried, dropping to my knees beside him. His eyes, usually so sharp and commanding, were clouded with pain and exhaustion.

He reached up suddenly, and my heart caught. Blood smeared across my face as his fingers pressed against my cheek. I flinched, but he didn't stop. He leaned closer, his lips brushing mine in a kiss that was both desperate and tender, sealing a promise in the chaos of the court.

"I killed him. I killed Maulgrove." I whispered, tears stinging my eyes.

"Powerful. I always knew you were," he rasped, a pained smile on his lips. "Even before...before you came, Liora...the trees...they whispered your name. I asked...I asked for you. I asked for a queen..."

I stared at him. An uncontrollable stare. His blood, his warmth, the raw intensity of his gaze—it anchored me.

"You were their answer," he continued, voice breaking with

effort. "I never imagined any human could face this madness and stand as you have. You...saved me. You saved us all."

Tears burned my cheeks, but I wiped them away, smearing fresh blood across my skin.

Corvin spoke, "You're the only one I would bleed for. The only one I would defy them all for."

"King Corvin." My voice barely held together.

He reached forward, brushing a strand of hair from my face. His fingers lingered, warm against my skin. "Yes?"

"Corvin Astravell. I command you to live."

He nodded slowly, a dark, knowing smile tugging at his lips. "For you, Liora, anything."

I held him tighter as his strength faltered, his head resting against my shoulder. In that quiet moment, it was as if only we existed, bound by survival, trust, and the quiet magic of whispered names carried on the wind.

CHAPTER 19
QUEEN OF NYRIATHEE

The chamber smelled faintly of smoke and herbs, the air heavy with candlewax and the tang of blood. Corvin lay against a mound of pillows, his skin a pale gray beneath the firelight, each breath shallow but stubbornly steady. I couldn't look at the bandages without remembering how close Tyvlen's blade had come to stealing him from me. How close we both had come to the end.

"You shouldn't be here," Corvin murmured, his voice rough as gravel. His eyes, though dulled by pain, found mine and softened. "And yet, I am glad you are."

I drew in a slow breath, my fingers tightening at my sides. "If I hadn't been there...if I hadn't taken your sword, then neither of us would have made it out of the Court of Starlight."

A faint smile ghosted across his lips, as though the effort cost him more than the words. "You wielded it as though it had always belonged to you. Perhaps one should."

His words struck deeper than I expected. I had only fought because I had no other choice, because he was falling and there was no one else. "I only did what I had to." But the memory burned in me still: Maulgrove's shadowed form lunging, my arms braced around Corvin's hilt, the blade tearing through Maulgrove's skin.

Corvin shifted slightly, grimacing. "And the arrow before from Esmara," he said, his voice lowering. "It fell from the ceiling—meant for you, not me. If it had struck..." He frowned, the faint lines on his brow deepening.

The chamber seemed to grow colder with the words spoken aloud. "Mimsy told me the faeries of Nyriathee were not happy to have me here," I admitted, my voice soft. "They've made comments and whispered terrible things. They say no human should be with their king."

Corvin's expression hardened. "What I do under my own rule is not the business of the Nyriathee Fae. I am king. I hold the power. I make my own rules."

"I understand," I whispered. "But after these attacks, it is clear I'm not supposed to be here. Not with you."

"Don't say that." His arm shifted with effort, his hand coming to rest gently against mine. Heat surged at the touch.

"You are meant to be here. I've asked the stars for you. The trees, this realm...it understands what you are to me. It feels the power you wield. Even if you don't."

My cheeks warmed, and I turned away. "A human and a half faerie king—"

"You don't need to be *only* human," he interrupted, voice steady, certain. "If you wish..."

I looked back at him sharply. "What do you mean by that?"

His faint smile faded, replaced by something heavier, unshakable. "I need a queen."

The word struck me like an arrow. *Queen*. It clung to my throat, sharp and foreign, impossible. My breath stuttered as the world seemed to tilt, the shadows of the chamber stretching long and heavy around us.

"Me?" I managed, rising to my feet as if distance could steady me. "I don't belong here...let alone on a throne."

Corvin's gaze did not waver. "Because you are different. Because I have seen you fight. I have seen you rise. No human has carried a sword as you did in the Court of Starlight. Your strength, your will... it is rare."

"That doesn't make me queen material," I said, though the words came weaker than I meant them to. "It just means I survived."

He leaned forward slightly, his voice low but unwavering. "There is more to being queen than bloodlines. You have a fire no other human has shown me. The power to change Nyriathee—not just with a blade, but with your spirit."

I shook my head, desperate to breathe past the storm in my chest. "I don't have magic like your people. I don't belong."

A wistful smile tugged at his lips. "That too can change." His eyes glimmered with something fierce. "I have seen the truth beneath your skin. Imagine what you could become with guidance. With Nyriathee's blood mingling with your own."

My heart thundered. The idea was unthinkable, terrifying... intoxicating. "You would change me?"

"Not to erase you," Corvin murmured. "To reveal you. To prepare you for the crown that is waiting—for the queen this realm already feels you are."

The weight of his words pressed down on me, heavy as steel, bright as fire. I wasn't ready. I might never be ready. Yet the moment had come, undeniable.

"Why me?" I whispered again, my voice barely more than a breath.

Corvin's gaze held mine, steady as iron. "Because you and I, together, are the future of Nyriathee."

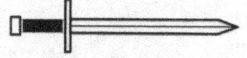

The wind blew softly through the trees, the air cool and calming as it brushed against my skin. Music drifted from the forest, faint and otherworldly, while the castle windows glowed with a soft pink light.

"Liora!" Elsie called. "The king would like to see you now!"

King Corvin Astrovell had finally healed from the attack in the Court of Starlight a few weeks ago. Corvin's presence was a shield, and he had trained me well enough to defend myself.

I had spent countless hours in the library, studying ways for a human to stand against the faeries of Nyriathee without relying on steel. Somewhere between those walls of ink and parchment, I had fallen in love with the knowledge, with the beauty of this world, and with the faeries themselves. They had begun to accept me, to see me not as an intruder but as someone worth welcoming. Some had even begun to love me, in the quiet, tentative way the king himself did.

"Miss Liora," King Corvin said as I entered, his voice warm. "I have missed seeing your face."

"I only went to the gardens for a walk," I laughed softly, smiling at him with nervous restraint.

"The gardens can wait," he replied, his gaze steady. "But this cannot."

Rising from his throne, Corvin stepped toward me. I drew in a breath, trying to quiet the anxious flutter in my chest.

"For you," he said, pulling a folded length of deep blue fabric from a carved chest. It was a gown, hand-stitched and luminous, scattered with sparkles that mirrored the stars above.

Words failed me. Its beauty silenced every thought.

Corvin draped it carefully over me, and it fit as though it had been sewn from the shape of my own shadow. Then he revealed a pair of boots, their surface shimmering in the dim firelight. I slipped them on, casting my worn shoes aside.

"And this..." His voice slowed, weighted. "Is for protection."

From a sheath, he drew a sword. Its blade caught the light, and its hilt, carved from bone, was etched with intricate vines and flowers found only in Nyriathee.

"It's beautiful," I whispered.

"As are you," he said, his gaze holding me captive. "But Liora, this is not just a weapon. It is a bond. The sword will answer only to you, and as it protects, so will I. Always."

My heart raced. The gown, the boots, the sword—it was as though he was reshaping me, clothing me not as a guest of the court, but as something more.

Corvin took a step closer, and before I could speak, he went down on one knee. The world seemed to still...the flickering torches, Elsie's excited giggles, even the faint music from the forest fading into silence.

"Liora," he said, his voice steady though his eyes betrayed a rare vulnerability. "Since the moment you fell into my world, you have carried both courage and kindness where others would have faltered. You have shielded me in ways no blade ever could. Will you stand beside me, not as a guest, not as a human passing through, but as my queen?"

The sword trembled in my hands, or perhaps it was my heart that trembled instead.

I opened my mouth, but words tangled in my throat. His eyes searched mine, dark and endless, filled with both power and a tenderness I had never thought possible from a king.

He spoke again, "Among all the celestial fires, it is your flame I seek, the only one that stirs what little remains of my heart."

My chest tightened, a mixture of awe and fear threatening to spill from me. The weight of the sword in my hands, the gown against my skin, the sparkle of the castle lights...everything seemed to draw me closer to him, yet I felt the enormity of the choice before me.

"I..." My voice faltered, but he gently lifted a hand to rest against my cheek, tilting my face toward him. His touch was warm, grounding, like the first sunlight after a long winter.

"Liora," he whispered, leaning just enough that I could feel the faint brush of his lips against my hand. "I do not ask you for your life, for your allegiance, or for anything less than yourself. Stand with me, as my queen, as the light that guides me through the shadows of this world."

Tears blurred my vision, but it was not sadness—it was wonder, awe, and a growing certainty. I looked down at the sword in my hands, then back at him, and I knew that this was more than a gift of protection; it was a promise, a bond, and the start of a life I had never dared imagine.

"Yes," I breathed, finally finding the words that had eluded me. "Yes, I will."

A slow, radiant smile spread across his face, and he rose, lifting me into a tight embrace. The castle around us shimmered, the pink glow of the windows deepening into a soft, golden light, as if even the walls themselves celebrated this moment.

"And together," he murmured, pressing his forehead to mine, "we will face whatever darkness comes, hand in hand, heart to heart."

I placed the sword in the new sheath that hung across my back as I nestled closer, feeling the warmth of his chest, the steady rhythm of his heartbeat. Around us, the music of the forest floated on the wind, as if the very world of Nyriathee had paused to witness this promise.

For the first time, I believed it. Not just in him, but in us, and in the world we could forge together. The sword gleamed softly, as though acknowledging our bond, while the stars above twinkled in silent applause.

And so, under the pink glow of the castle and the watchful eyes of the Nyriathee, our story began anew—two hearts united, a human, and a half-faerie, with a love that would burn brighter than any celestial fire.

King Corvin Astravell and Queen Liora Astravell. Rulers Of Nyriathee and the Court of Starlight.